By the same author

Meanwhile Back at the Ranch

Steppin' on a Rainbow

The Mile High Club

Spanking Watson

Blast from the Past

Roadkill

The Love Song of J. Edgar Hoover

God Bless John Wayne

Armadillos & Old Lace

Elvis, Jesus & Coca Cola

Musical Chairs

Frequent Flyer

When the Cat's Away

A Case of Lone Star

Greenwich Killing Time

THE PRISONER OF VANDAM STREET

A NOVEL

KINKY FRIEDMAN

Simon & Schuster

New York   London   Toronto   Sydney

SIMON & SCHUSTER
Rockefeller Center
1230 Avenue of the Americas
New York, NY 10020

SIMON & SCHUSTER and colophon are registered trademarks
of Simon & Schuster, Inc.

For information regarding special discounts for bulk purchases,
please contact Simon & Schuster Special Sales at
1-800-456-6798 or business@simonandschuster.com

Designed by Lauren Simonetti

Manufactured in the United States of America

1   3   5   7   9   10   8   6   4   2

Library of Congress Cataloging-in-Publication Data
Friedman, Kinky.
The prisoner of Vandam Street / Kinky Friedman.
p. cm.
1. Private investigators—New York (State)—New York—Fiction. 2. SoHo (New York,
N.Y.)—Fiction. 3. Malaria—Patients—Fiction. 4. Witnesses—Fiction. I. Title.

PS3556.R527P75 2004
813'.54—dc22   2003065906
ISBN 0-7432-4602-0

This book is dedicated to The Friedmans:
Perky, Mr. Magoo, Brownie, and Chumley.
May you faithfully help to carry the
Friedman family name into the future.

"Steal your tomorrows and live them today."

—Will Hoover, "Sweet Lady Jane,"
The Lost Outlaw Album

"Find what you like and let it kill you."

—Leon "Slim" Dodson

Chapter One

Nobody can stay in the middle forever and it was becoming increasingly clear to me, the longer I knew him, that McGovern was losing it. By it, I did not mean his wit, his health, his sex drive, or even his mind. All of those faculties, as near as I cared to tell, seemed to be as intact as was humanly possible in a person like McGovern. But the it he appeared to be losing, unfortunately, was something even more deleterious to his interpersonal relations, the brunt of which, I hasten to point out, fell squarely upon the shoulders of a man already burdened with far too many earthly responsibilities, namely myself. What McGovern was losing, though he did not realize it himself, was his hearing.

Now, I'm not making light of people who are deaf or losing their hearing. I am not mocking a disability that afflicts millions of

Americans as they grow older, effectively cutting them off to varying degrees from the hearing world. All I'm saying, and I'll try to speak loudly and slowly and enunciate clearly, is that they should get medical help or a hearing aid or a large, metal ear-horn like the kind that was used in medieval times, and stop constantly blaming hapless, sensitive friends like myself for mumbling. I do not mumble; I vocalize with intensity and tonality not dissimilar to the shriek of a parrot on the shoulder of an altar boy out bird-watching with the cardinal. The only person I've ever met who's been inherently unable or unwilling to understand me is Mike McGovern and I believe he enjoys the high degree of frustration he engenders in his listening audience, which, fortunately for you, is usually me. So while McGovern may technically be the party with the medical malady, as time goes by, I increasingly see myself as the victim.

What I find particularly maddening about McGovern is that, instead of doing something to help his condition, he instead chooses to incessantly repeat the phrase, "Say again?" Compounding the tedium of this mortal, yet irritating crutch, is that McGovern, being a veteran journalist, first in Chicago and then in New York, is one of the most prying, inquisitive creatures on the planet, and one who fashions his entire system of communication in the form of questions. So McGovern proceeds to interrogate his prey ad nauseam, and then, as the innocent victim dutifully answers every question in an endless stream of verbiage, with almost every answer, McGovern follows up with, "Say again?" This ingrained behavior makes a short conversation virtually impossible, a longer conversation interminable, and any conversation

2

unpleasant. The whole situation is usually not improved upon by the fact that McGovern is invariably drinking during almost all forms of human intercourse.

Thus it was mildly ironic that McGovern, one of the most irritating of that irritating group of men known as the Village Irregulars, was soon to become my primary care-giver in a nightmare scenario I never could've dreamed up. When you're in the business I'm in, of course, you don't worry much about irritation. Irritation comes with the territory—like evil, ennui, and cat turds, in a random and haphazard order. As a private investigator in the City of New York, you come to depend upon those whom you consider your friends, even if they are sometimes unreliable, unredeemable, and, in one case I can think of, unhygienic. You are a mender of human destinies. Your work can often be a matter of life or death for your client, yourself, your associates, or for someone who may be a completely innocent bystander. Fortunately, there are very few completely innocent bystanders in New York.

It all started, as near as I can recall, one seemingly normal night in the dead of winter. McGovern and I were inhabiting two barstools at the Corner Bistro, maintaining a low-key celebration of a case I'd wrapped up fairly recently. As things had transpired, McGovern had played a rather constructive, not insignificant role in resolving the investigation. He had fought several pitched battles with his editor at the *Daily News,* emerged triumphant in both of them, and written two major features involving my quest to find a small autistic boy who'd gone missing in the city. New York is not a small town in Kansas. For an amateur private investigator to have any luck here, he has to rely upon the help and good will of

3

others. In other words, if you have to have a friend, he might as well be in the media.

The kid's name was Dylan Weinberg. His nanny was an old black woman named Hattie Mamajello. His father was an asshole. His half-sister was gorgeous, a fact that almost derailed the usually peerless detecting ability of my sometimes partner, Steve Rambam. The kid, though brilliant, had a rather limited vocabulary, consisting, in fact, of only one word. The word was "shnay." In the end, it was enough to solve the case.

"Shnay," I said to McGovern.

"Say again?" he said.

"Shnay," I said again, a little louder, looking up with mild irritation from my third pint of Guinness.

"Shea?" said McGovern, looking up blamelessly from his fourth Vodka McGovern. "The stadium?"

"Shnay!" I said viciously, and loudly enough to turn the heads of several nearby patrons.

"You don't have to shout," shouted McGovern petulantly. "I can hear you!"

We drank for a while in a state of sullen silence. Either we were heroic friends or we were stuck with each other and either one was bad enough. However, there was no reason to let little things put a strain on a relationship that was already hanging by spit. I didn't want McGovern to go into one of his famous McGovern snits, so I made the first overture.

"We've been through a lot together," I said wistfully.

McGovern turned his barstool toward me. He leaned his large head closer and looked me right in the eyes.

"Say again?" he said.

It was sad really. On the other hand, what the hell difference did it really make? Most of the people in the world drank a lot less than McGovern and their sense of hearing was far superior, yet they went through life never really understanding, never really listening to anybody anyway. McGovern, I thought, was like a big, autistic child. He'd never grown up; he'd just gotten older. If you had a few pints of Guinness and thought about it for a while, it was kind of admirable.

"Remember the first time we met?" said McGovern.

"Yeah," I said. "Didn't Piers Akerman introduce us?"

"That's right." McGovern laughed with his big Irish laugh. "In the closet of your suite during that wild party at the Essex House."

"We're the only two men in New York who ever went *into* the closet," I said.

It was amazing, I thought. McGovern had maintained an entire snatch of conversation without losing the thread and without saying "Say again?" Maybe he was some kind of meditational guru who'd trained himself only to hear things in which he was interested. Maybe he was in touch with some form of high spirituality like a dog or cat who could detect the essence and the meaning of things without needing to hear the words. Maybe he was akin to George Bernard Shaw, a fellow Irishman, who reportedly had such native sensitivity that he could review a play without even having to see it.

"Maybe you *are* a genius," I said.

"I'm drowning in sarcasm," said McGovern.

"No, I'm serious. You have the uncanny, childlike ability to hear

5

when you want to hear and not hear when you don't want to hear."

"What?" said McGovern. "Say again?"

"I'm not going to say *anything* again!" I said very loudly.

"I heard you!" shouted McGovern angrily. "You don't have to shout! You don't have to make a scene! Life knows you better than you know yourself!"

It was at this point that I began feeling decidedly strange. I'd been experiencing some chills in the past few days and now they seemed to be coming home for their class reunion. I was not only literally contorting with the shaking chills, but I also seemed to be breathing rapidly and sweating profusely. Suddenly the whole place seemed hot as hell.

"God," I said. "I feel like I'm burning up with fever."

"Say again?" said McGovern, signaling the bartender for another round, totally oblivious to my condition.

". . . burning . . . up . . . with . . . *fever*," I managed to stammer.

"What?" said McGovern. "Let's get some *beaver?*"

I must have passed out because when I came to again, the Corner Bistro was gone, the whole world was bathed in a sickly envelope of white, and I thought I was dead. It would require six more weeks for me to wish I were.

CHAPTER TWO

Where the hell's Saint Peter?" I said. "I'm not going to sit here on this cloud playing a harp for all eternity! I didn't sign up for this shit!"

"Settle down, Kinkster," said a familiar voice. "You're not in heaven nor are you ever bloody likely to be. But don't you fret yourself. I'll save you a seat down there, mate."

The voice sounded either Irish or cockney, and to my tin American ear it seemed as if it must have been emanating from the kind of person Professor Higgins might be fascinated with. It was oddly calming, however, because I was on the edge of panic thinking about what I might or might not see when I opened my eyes.

I opened my eyes.

What a joke. I wasn't in heaven or hell, just in the same mortal limbo most of us have experienced all our lives as we crawl toward the stars, inch forward in traffic, circle a bug light with weather-beaten wings, love someone who does not love us in return.

"Bollocks!" shouted the voice again. "I've spilt the fuckin' coffee!"

I was lying on a small bed in a pool of my own sweat in a small white room. The lighting appeared to be set at a level of high interrogation.

"What a fuckin' load of cobblers!" shouted the voice angrily. "Dress me up in ermine."

I looked over and saw the friendly, if somewhat aggravated features of my friend Mick Brennan. Mick was one of the best photographers in the world. He was also one of the best troublemakers.

"There was no reason for McGovern to have done that," I said evenly.

"McGovern's a total wanker," said Brennan. "Bloke like that could've done anything."

"Not this."

"What'd he do?"

I thought about it for a moment. I still couldn't believe it. But it was the most obvious possible explanation for the unpleasant circumstances in which I now found myself. I did not want to tell Brennan what I suspected, so I answered his question, in Talmudic fashion, with another question. Maybe, like many Talmudic scholars, I was just a little confused myself. It sometimes happens to you when you think you're getting close to God.

"What are you doing here?" I said.

"I'm here, aren't I?" said Brennan.

"You would've made a good Talmudic scholar yourself if you hadn't been raised an Irish Protestant."

"I was working under cover for the Catholics, mate."

"There's only one Catholic I'd like you to work on for me: McGovern. I'd like you to kill him."

"The McGoverns are a dodgy lot, mate, aren't they? But why'd you want to kill the tosser? After all, it was McGovern who called me and asked me to come here to the hospital to look after you."

"It all fits," I said.

"You're talkin' rubbish, mate. McGovern was—well, he was walkin' on his knuckles, mate. He'd been on the piss for six days and he must've thought it was a week. I mean, I'm not defending McGovern—"

"Good, because he tried to kill me."

"Mate, it's not logical, is it? If he'd wanted to croak you, why'd he bring you here to St. Vincent's? Why'd he call me to come look after you? He was just lookin' out for you, mate. That's the way it is, innit?"

"I think he was just covering his tracks. I think he slipped me a mickey at the Corner Bistro."

"Now why would he want to do that, mate? Besides, McGovern's so big he'd need a bleedin' domed stadium to cover his tracks. You're just a wee bit crook, mate. That's the way it is, innit? That's why I'm here, aren't I? I talked to the head sawbones. Caught up with him in the hallway. Says they're runnin' tests on your blood. We'll soon know what the problem is, won't we?"

"So you seem to think McGovern's innocent?"

9

"'Course he is, mate. The only thing he's guilty of is being a total wanker."

"You're right. McGovern and I were drinking in the Corner Bistro and we had some rather tedious tension convention—I can't remember what it was about—and I started shivering and sweating and feeling like I was going to begin squirtin' out of both ends—"

"Well, you're in the right place now, aren't you?"

There was something irritating about the cockney custom of tacking the little question to the end of every sentence. It was also beginning to sound rather patronizing, as if Brennan were speaking to a child or an idiot or a grievously ill person. Was I any of the above, I wondered? Of course not. Whatever anybody said about McGovern, he didn't have a mean bone in his large body. No way would he have done anything so dastardly and devious as to land me in the horsepital. I told Mick Brennan as much.

"You know, Mick," I said, "now that I think about it, there's no way McGovern would've ever slipped me a mickey."

"You're right, mate. You want to know what I think?"

"Do I have a choice? I'm here, trapped in this horsepital bed, freezing my ass off, drowning in sweat—"

"We haven't had a wet dream, have we?"

"—listening to you natter away about what *you* think. I want to know what the hell's wrong with me! What does the head sawbones, as you call him, think?"

"He's probably on the golf course by now, mate. We have to be patient, don't we? Slowly, slowly, catchee monkey, innit?"

I was really starting to not feel well again. The fever and the chills and the nausea seemed to be coming in waves, taking me far out into a dark and turbulent sea, floating me in and out of consciousness. Whatever affliction was afflicting me, I figured it wasn't going to be any walk in Central Park. Just judging from the way I felt, whatever I had, had me better than I had it. It felt like I'd just gone ten rounds with death's little sister, to paraphrase Hemingway who I think was talking about fame, which, of course, is always a death of a sort. If my fans could only see me now, I thought. I could use some fans, actually, the propeller type. The fucking place was burning up.

I must've nodded out, 'cause when I woke up Brennan was gone. This did not surprise me terribly. Mick was not the most reliable of the Village Irregulars. He was certainly one of the most charming, though, but when you're lying at death's door, alternately freezing your ass off or burning to death, charm has its limitations. I knew instinctively now that what was wrong with me was more than someone slipping me a mickey. People lie to you when you're sick. Your friends tend to sugarcoat things. Doctors often tell you what they think you want to hear. The best gauge of how well you are or how sick you are, whether you're in a horsepital or out of one, is always yourself. Myself was grudgingly, yet ruthlessly telling me that I was an extremely sick chicken. I did not take the news very well.

A nurse came in a couple of times and each time I asked her what I had, what was wrong with me. Each time she said she didn't know. She said when the tests came back from the lab the doctor would tell me. I asked her when that would be. She said she didn't know.

11

I tried to sleep, but it's not easy when your forehead feels hotter than the third ring of Saturn. Or was it Jupiter that had the rings? When you're delirious, it's hard to remember these things. When you're healthy, they may assume a certain degree of importance in a game of trivia or a college exam or some other exercise in vapidity. But when you're dying, you really don't give a damn. Dr. Seuss may be painting rings on Joan of Arc's anus and it'd work for you. When you're dying, as my friend Speed Vogel says, your heart attack is everybody else's hangnail. This applies even if you only think you're dying. Sometimes that's enough to enlighten you if you ever had any doubts about the fragility of the spider webs of friendship and the fatuous, superficial, pathetic nature of human beings in general. Most of the time we're not even good enough to be evil. We do things, even good and great things, almost always because, consciously or unconsciously, it suits us to do them. Not that I was expecting Mick Brennan to donate his kidney to me. I wasn't even sure if I wanted Mick Brennan's kidney. I was sure I didn't want his liver. Anyway, when you're dying or think you're dying, it's the people and the animals and the places long ago and far away that always seem the closest to your heart. Everybody and everything else around you sucks hind teat compared with them. And the closer your dearest distant dreams become, the closer you are to death. I was dreaming of the time when my eleven-year-old nephew, David, sneezed on the entire left side of the beautifully presented lox and bagel buffet. Into this cherished moment the sounds of an altercation intruded themselves quite cacophonously. Whatever was happening appeared to be happening right in my horsepital room.

"Sir!" said a stern female voice. "You can't bring that in here."

"Shite!" said a voice I recognized as Brennan's. "I'm behavin' meself, aren't I? This is America, innit?"

"There is *no* alcohol allowed in the hospital, sir!"

"What about rubbing alcohol, you silly cow? I was here before, wasn't I? Just popped over to the pub, didn't I? What is this? A poofter operation? Scratch the word 'operation,' luv. I misspoke meself. Don't want to disturb a dyin' bloke—I mean a *sick* bloke—"

"Nurse," I said, shivering under several blankets, "are the tests back from the lab yet?"

"What tests?" said the nurse.

"The bleedin' blood tests!" shouted Brennan. "The sawbones is supposed to come tell us, innit he?"

"The doctor has gone home for the day," said the nurse coldly. "He will be here at seven o'clock in the morning by which time I trust this gentleman will be gone."

"Now wait a minute, you ol' boiler!" shouted Brennan belligerently. "Just who you callin' a gentleman?"

Sometime later, after the nurse had driven off in a 1937 snit, I started feeling hot again, kicked the blankets off, then tried to get up and find my pants. As I sat up in bed, the room began swirling around me like a galaxy that had taken mescaline. I lay back down in the hell of my sweaty bed, waiting for a doctor who might or might not show up with test results or no test results at seven in the morning. I had no idea if it was night or day, but seven in the morning seemed an eternity away.

The fever, if anything, appeared to be getting worse. Wildly contemplating what was wrong with me was pushing me to the edge of panic. It was at that point that I heard Brennan's words wash over me. They were spoken from his chair beside my bed, sadly, softly, and sincerely, almost, indeed, as if he were speaking to himself.

"No, McGovern didn't slip you a mickey," he said. "I'll tell you what I think happened."

"What?" I said weakly.

"I think somebody put a curse on you, mate."

"Why don't we wait for the lab tests?"

"Why don't we wait for the pubs to open?"

We waited. I looked at Brennan. He tried to smile, but I could see that he was a deeply worried man. That made two of us. Before I passed out again I saw a grove of banana trees, a sacred hornbill bird, and a group of little brown children playing beside a coffee-colored river.

Chapter Three

By all rights and all wrongs, I should've died that night, and there've been times, gentile reader, when I wish I had. Does it make that much difference to the world when another bright little spark goes out in the eye of a stray on the busy corner of truth and vermouth? I'm wearing the shirt my father died in and his arm is coming out of my sleeve. Is there anyone awake tonight in this little town or was it already dead before the virus hit? In that calm, reflective rage that inevitably comes to us all, I think we can agree that our lives are works of fiction, and that it hardly matters in what manner you lived or died or shat through a typewriter. Just assume, gentile reader, that we are walking in single file through the united nations of hell and you are walking slightly ahead of the character but slightly behind the author and then the author conks on page fifty-seven leaving only you and the character to fight it out over a few scraps of imagination. "But what happened to the mystery?" some discerning reader may no doubt remark. "What happened to the mystery of life?" We'll get to that in a moment. Right now we have a dead author on our hands, and like all dead authors he gets better with time. And like all living authors, he knew that all he really wanted was fame and immortality, and like all dead authors he knows that it's a trade-off and that the less you usually get of the former the more you often receive of the latter, if you follow meeeeeee, which you probably don't. Not that I'm Jesus or anybody; I'm just another dead author looking for the right place to use a semicolon and aspiring to inspire before I expire which happily is never too late for a dead author. But now the editor who has just returned from a busy night of air-kissing Michael Jackson's publicist at a cocktail party is scanning this shit and thinks he detects a slight change in the tonality which could either be a literary cry for help or a trendy new writing style that the casual critic might mistake for serious writing. It's kind of a refreshing change from the formulaic mystery format, and what the hell, it's only mildly insulting to the reader who might conceivably realize that he may have a dead author on his hands and sure as shit doesn't want to see the fictional character killed off as well, so the editor e-mails the publisher, and while the dead author and his fucking typewriter are drifting off to hell through the torporous Texas night, he brings in a cold nephew from a blue prison or a well-intentioned highly alliterative asshole to complete the work after the fashion that a respectable cult of readers around the world has come to know and love. Like all good editors, the editor resents the author, and the publisher doesn't care about the editor or the author, both of whom resent the publisher, and the author, like all good authors, writes with a total disregard for the reader, who, like all good lovers, loves the heart who doesn't love him, and everybody hates Hollywood. The publisher thinks he owns all this shit, but he doesn't. It's a borrowed campfire.

Most Americans should've probably skipped this chapter, anyway, but fortunately we're too busy driving vehicles, taking dumps, whacking off all at the same time, and we're afraid we missed something in the back-story. Or we might be sharper than that, and we might jump through our asshole and shout, "What asshole published this shit? What asshole edited this shit? What asshole wrote this shit?" And the dead author would probably say, "Me and my fucking typewriter are saving you a seat in hell because you're the asshole who's reading this shit." And, you know, they'd all be right. That's the way it is, innit?

CHAPTER FOUR

In life, I've always thought, it's a good thing to practice waking up in hell because then, when the real thing comes, you'll be ready for it. While it was true that Mick Brennan's Irish-cockney style and rather blunt interpersonal techniques were cloying and somewhat tedious, they were far less maddening than McGovern's pecking you to death with "Say again?"

Moving from McGovern to Brennan, I felt, was like traveling up to a higher circle of hell. The next auditory sensation I experienced, however, convinced me beyond any doubt that I had plunged to new depths and was currently residing inside the very bowels of that fiery and terrible place.

"Kinkstah!!" shouted the familiar rodentlike voice, far too loud and ebullient for the way my mind and body were feeling.

"Kinkstah! I'm here, baby! Your favorite Doctor! Doctor Watson, of course!"

"Ratso," I said weakly. "Could you turn down your vocal mike?"

"Sure, Kinkstah! Anything, Kinkstah! I came as soon as Brennan called me. He was in some pub run by a friend of his who kept it open all night because Mick was suffering from post-traumatic stress disorder. Said something was seriously wrong with you resulting from complications brought about by McGovern slipping you a mickey at the Corner Bistro. I knew that couldn't be it, Kinkstah. What's really wrong with you, Kinkstah?"

"Munchausen by proxy. I want to kill all of the Village Irregulars."

"That's technically not the correct definition of munchausen by proxy, Sherlock. In munchausen by proxy, the primary care-giver—I'm your primary care-giver, by the way—"

"That's comforting."

"—could be a mother, a nurse, a nanny, someone like that. Anyway, the primary care-giver seeks to make the child sick or appear to be sick either physically or emotionally so that the care-giver gets attention or sympathy by extension—"

"Ah, you're so insightful, Watson! Only a keen, observant mind like yours would have the insight to realize my malady for what it is—a cry for help. That's all it is. An attention-getting device. The fact that my temperature's a hundred and six and that I'm alternately freezing to death or burning alive, and that I'm shitting and pissing and puking and delirious and hallucinating—"

"Get a grip on yourself, Sherlock. No one's saying you're not sick. We all realize you're sick—"

"And I realize that you're sick—"

"And you're the one shivering in a hospital bed with a face that looks like a death mask. But don't worry, Sherlock. We'll find out what's wrong with you and have you back on your feet in no time! I just saw the doctor down the hall. He's coming in to check on you soon."

"What does he look like?"

"A waiter at the Bengali Palace."

"Why does every guy from India always come to New York and wind up being a doctor?"

"Because they couldn't figure out how to drive a taxi?"

There were times when a little light banter with Ratso might have amused me, but this was not one of them. Here he was laughing and yapping away, and every time I closed my eyes I saw a pale horse. Or a coffee-colored river. There may have been times in my life when my grasp on mortality was more tenuous, but I couldn't remember when. This could really be it, I reflected darkly. This was the way the world ends, not with a bang but with Ratso nattering away about the precise definition of munchausen by proxy, or Brennan calling the nurse an ol' boiler or McGovern a wanker. Where was McGovern, by the way? A little strange, wasn't it? I no longer believed he'd slipped me a mickey, but I figured he'd at least pop in to see what condition my condition was in. Maybe I was imagining things, but I was beginning to see a troubled, sadly vexed visage lurking just beneath the bright countenance of Ratso's face. This troubled me too and vexed me not a little. If Ratso was worried, it was no doubt about a quarter past the time for me to be worried because, after all, I was the one who was

21

hanging by spit directly above the trapdoor. One of the most depressing things about being in a horsepital terribly afflicted with a very serious, very mysterious ailment, is watching people pretend that it's nothing serious. There is a gravestone I once saw in the bone orchard called Shalom Memorial Park just outside of Chicago where my mother and father are buried. The gravestone has the man's name and dates of birth and death, and underneath those particulars it simply reads: "Nothing serious." There's another gravestone there that is inscribed with something in Yiddish, underneath which the translation is thoughtfully included: "The Cubs stink."

I seemed to be enjoying a brief respite from the fever and the shaking chills, but there was to be no respite, apparently, from Ratso. He was wandering back and forth, constantly moving from the room to the hallway, waiting for the doctor, all the while eating the breakfast that I couldn't eat and yammering away about this and that. The current subject of his yapping, as near as I could tell, appeared to be the physical attributes of a young woman he'd met at the nurse's station.

"Jesus," he shouted. "You should've seen the rack on that broad! She was kind of hysterical though. Her mother's very sick, I think."

"Everybody here is very sick, Ratso. That's why we call it a hospital."

"Anyway, I didn't get her phone number."

"That's a shame."

The conversation was sapping what little energy I had. Not only that, but the nausea now was coming in waves that also appeared to blur my vision and my thought processes as well. My auditory

22

senses seemed to be fine, but it was not a pleasant prospect that Ratso might have to become not only my eyes but also my voice to the rational world, if indeed, such a place existed. At least Ratso was loyal, I thought. He positively luxuriated in playing Dr. Watson to my Sherlock. If at times he could be a pluperfect asshole, at least he was a fixed pluperfect asshole in a changing age. Now if he only was possessed with Watson's medical abilities.

"Watson," I said, half-deliriously.

"Yes, Sherlock," said Ratso with genuine concern. "What is it?"

"Watson," I said. "What if I'm dying?"

"You can't die, Sherlock," he said. "You're only on chapter four."

"Ah, Watson! How practical of you to make that observation."

"And I'd like to make another observation," Ratso sang out cheerfully. "Here comes the doctor now!"

I looked up and saw a small man as thin and dark as a pencil standing before me and wavering like a mirage on a summer highway. Once my eyes focused a bit I realized that he did look a great deal like a waiter at the Bengali Palace. I found this oddly comforting. The doctor studied my chart assiduously for about six hours, stared at me balefully for about a fortnight, then, as I began sinking into a state of torporous confusion again, he spoke at last.

"'Ello, my name is Dr. Q. Tip Skinnipipi," he said, in an accent thicker than mulligatawny soup. "What you have, my dear fellow, is malaria."

"Malaria!" shrieked Ratso, in a voice that might not have wakened the dead, but certainly would have irritated them. "Where in the hell did he get malaria?"

I followed the conversation but I did not seem able to form

23

words or even wish to participate. Had I been able to speak, how-ever, I probably would've asked the same question Ratso had.

"Malaria is quite rare in America these days," said Skinnipipi. "Quite rare, indeed. Has the patient come into contact recently with any migrant workers' camps?"

"The patient," said Ratso, "has never worked a day in his life."

"I see," said Skinnipipi gravely. I was glad that somebody could see. The doctor's face was now resembling an old rugged cross between Gunga Din and a child's Halloween mask as glimpsed through a rearview carnival mirror on a 1944 Jesus H. Christler as it sailed over some crazy cliff into Armadillo Canyon. Even I, as the patient, could sort of half-tell that I was delirious at the moment. In an offbeat way it was kind of fun listening to the adults discuss my condition in serious grown-up tones, as if I were a child who wasn't there. I liked the way Dr. Skinnipipi rolled the "r" in the word "malaria." I was hoping he would do it again. As it hap-pened, I didn't have long to wait.

"There are four different strains of human malarrria, you see," said Dr. Skinnipipi instructionally to Ratso. "They are caused by four different species of the Plasmodium parasite."

"Got it," said Ratso, as he took copious notes in a little notepad. In my experience, I've never really trusted people who said "Got it." It usually means they don't get it.

"The patient may have contracted malarrrrrria many years ago," Skinnipipi droned on. "It may have persisted in the liver and recurred. We do not know, you see. Even if the patient may know the answer, we cannot expect a coherent response for forty-eight hours, when the fever breaks."

"MamaMAmamamama!" I said.

"Got it," said Ratso. "By the way, doctor, what are the four strains of malaria?"

"They are *Plasmodium vivax, Plasmodium ovale, Plasmodium fuckmedeadmate,* and the last, and only truly deadly strain, *Plasmodium falciparum.*"

"Got it," said Ratso, scribbling furiously. "Which strain does the patient have?"

"*Plasmodium falciparum,*" said Skinnipipi.

"Beedledeedee!" I said.

"And that would be—" said Ratso, looking over his notes.

"—the only truly deadly strain," finished the doctor smoothly.

Ratso, for once, was silent. The patient, as near as I could tell, was silent. Indeed, for that moment in time, all the sirens and subways and cell phones and dogs and babies and junkies in New York seemed suddenly muted by a cosmic finger. And, even in my state of fevered delirium, I suspected I knew which finger it was.

At last, the doctor spoke again. This time he spoke directly to Ratso. He spoke in a soft, hushed tone, almost as if I was not lying there in a hospital bed but had already begun my journey, winding my way to heaven, or hell, or very possibly, to nowhere at all.

"As you would say," said Dr. Skinnipipi rather officiously, "he has 'got it.'"

CHAPTER FIVE

McGovern surfaced about the time my fever broke. I was not pleased to discover that I was still in the same dreary hospital room, but I figured it was preferable to being on a cloud somewhere playing a fucking harp. I'd missed McGovern, actually, and the truth was he represented a very comforting force as he sat in a large comfortable chair by my bed, reading a newspaper and reminding me by his very presence that I was still alive.

"Hell of a hangover," he said, laughing loudly at his own little joke. The sound of that Irish laughter, I must report, while not quite music to my ear, was not at all unpleasant.

"We'll beat this thing, Kink," he said with unbridled gentile optimism. "Ratso apprised me of the full situation."

"Where is Ratso?" I said.

"He left a few hours ago. Said he had to take a powder."

"With Ratso that could mean any number of things," I muttered.

"What about 'wings'?" asked McGovern. "Say again?"

"I said, 'Ratso doesn't pull any strings.'"

"None of us do, Kinkster. We're all on your side and we're all going to do everything we can to get you better."

"Then it's just possible that I'm really fucked," I observed bleakly.

"What? You think the hospital really sucks? I wouldn't say that, Kink. Of course, they did throw Brennan out of here last night, but the shape he was in he probably would've gotten 86'ed at the Monkey's Paw. I think this hospital's really been good to you, Kink."

"So has baseball."

"Say again? What about baseball?"

"Nothing."

"No, you can *tell* me. I can *hear* you. Just stop mumbling and *say* it."

"I said, 'I'd like to throw a baseball at your scrotum!'"

"Modem?" said McGovern brightly. "You're getting a new modem?"

And so the conversation went. Like millions of other conversations between husbands and wives, lawyers and whores, hunters and hunted, full of all the words Andy Gibb ever had, full of horseshit and wild honey, full of sound and fury, signifying only the meaninglessness of life. Yet even without the words and the music, life did occasionally convey a flying scrap of reckless wonder from the kind heart of a large Irishman to the tattered soul of a fevered Jew. There are people, I thought, not for the first time,

28

there are people. And the beauty of it was you never knew who they would be. Old friends, perfect strangers, even pluperfect assholes, all might catch you in the wink of an eye, call your name like a train whistle in the night, guide you like an angel on your shoulder. There were people, I thought. And one of them was sitting in a chair in a hospital room reading a newspaper.

"Ratso's worried," said McGovern, looking up from the paper, "but I'm not. You're tough, Kink. Or you wouldn't have gotten this far."

"I guess I have done pretty well for myself," I said, glancing around the depressing little room. "I've got a sink and a urinal. What more could I ask for?"

"I don't even know why you need both," said McGovern.

"You might be right."

"What? Need more light?" McGovern got up and turned the room lighting on to high interrogation. It flooded the room with fluorescent light and blinded me.

"You sure you want more light?" asked McGovern solicitously.

"I'm not sure of anything," I said.

Time drifted by as it tends to do in horsepitals, airports, whorehouses, train stations, slaughter yards; it drifted by like a hobo in the night, so slowly, so swiftly, so silently that you almost forgot it was there. Little minutes, little moments, little pieces of our lives that no one's ever sure quite what to do with. The present blends with the past and the faraway becomes suddenly very close to the heart and the lost and distant are suddenly near and dear and the pearly shells on the childhood beach are the bright, dead leaves in the old man's yard. When I came to again I wasn't certain if moments had passed or years, but there was a large, Jewish buttocks obscuring my line of vision and, from previous sightings, I

29

took it to be Ratso's. He, apparently, was engaged in a serious discussion with McGovern, who, I assumed, was standing on the other side of the buttocks.

"So tell me more about this Dr. Pickaninny," McGovern was saying.

"It's Dr. Skinnipipi," Ratso corrected, "and he says there's good news and bad news."

"That's what they all say," I said.

Ratso and McGovern looked over at me, as if I'd just risen from the dead. A nurse was checking an IV line that was dripping into my arm. For the first time in what seemed like ages, my mind felt clear and lucid. I knew who I was and where I was and then it became confused with the recent blurry past and I lost the moment of precious clarity and watched it disappear like a lover on a train. Now the place was filled with the dim forms of people and animals I had loved and known in my life, some of them I knew to be still alive, some I knew to have long ago and quite recently departed this busy station of mortal sadness.

"What are all these people doing in my room?" I said.

Ratso and McGovern exchanged worried glances. They came closer to my bed. Ratso spoke softly, an event that occurred only on very rare occasions. I knew I was in trouble.

"They're here because they love you," he said.

"Oh," I said. And I closed my eyes.

This is when I learned the great secret of life and death: When you close your eyes, the living disappear, but the dead keep on living. So I traded one Ratso and one McGovern for everyone else I'd ever loved and lost. It was a good trade, actually, but it wasn't quite enough to win the pennant.

CHAPTER SIX

Unfortunately, Jim the Ferry Boatman on Vancouver Island refused to punch my ticket to the Grateful Dead concert. My number wasn't up yet, apparently, so I had to go on living whether I wanted to or not. Reflecting back on those close moments, I don't think I really wanted to die. I just wanted a little time away from Ratso and McGovern. That's not asking so fucking much, is it? I mean I wouldn't have minded dying, and I probably will die some day, but at the time I had a few projects I was working on and frankly I was getting damn tired of leaving the cat with the lesbians upstairs. If I kept doing that, the cat was going to turn into a lesbian, and if there's one thing everybody hates it's a lesbian cat.

Yet the health, education, and welfare of the cat had been nagging at me quite a bit lately. People tend not to be too concerned about other people's pets unless they vomit in your shoes or bite you in the ass. I'd already been in the horsepital for several days, and there was no sign I could detect that I was improving or about to be discharged, and if I left it up to Ratso and McGovern to remember to take care of the cat, there'd be a small set of skeletal remains to greet me when and if I ever returned to 199B Vandam Street.

I vowed that if I ever opened my eyes again and returned to what we like to think of as consciousness, I'd make sure in no un-certain terms that either Ratso or McGovern went right over to the loft and fed the cat. Whether the cat should be taken upstairs to Winnie Katz's was an open question. Would it be better to have the cat neglected by the Village Irregulars or corrupted by Winnie? That's what it all came down to. And I could just imagine what the loft looked like. The cat by this time would be setting about in a fe-line fugue, vindictively dumping on everything I held dear. There would no doubt be cat shit on my pillow, cat shit on the espresso machine, cat shit on the two blowers, cat shit on the puppethead, cat shit on Sherlock Holmes's head. Some day scientists would probably discover that the world was made of cat shit. Probably the moon was made of cat shit. Pâté was made of cat shit. Einstein was made of cat shit. Princess Di was made of cat shit. Mother Teresa was made of cat shit. Jerry Lewis was made of cat shit. Gibraltar was made of cat shit. Mt. Everest was made of cat shit. Palestine was made of cat shit. The pope was made of cat shit. Jesus was made of cat shit. God was made of cat shit. Peter Jennings was made of cat shit. Scientists will some day discover that all of mankind is made of cat shit except for one man. That man is John

Ashcroft. Scientists will some day discover that John Ashcroft is made of horseshit. Just another reason not to open your eyes.

"Kinkstah! Kinkstah!" shouted Ratso. "Leap sideways, Kinkstah!"

I opened my eyes. Ratso's large head darted away from me, soon to be magically replaced by McGovern's even larger head. It looked like a very bad puppet show.

"Kink!" said McGovern, with all the excitement of a small child at Christmastime. "Dr. Pickaninny's here!"

"Audrey Hepburn's made of cat shit," I said.

Like two pistons in the engine of humanity, McGovern's head disappeared again, only to be replaced once more by Ratso's head, his frightening face smiling like an idiot.

"Dr. Skinnipipi's got something to tell you, Kinkstah!" he shouted.

"John Wayne's made of cat shit," I said.

"Poor fellow's obviously delirious," said Dr. Skinnipipi, "but that's to be expected with malarrrrria—"

"Eleanor Roosevelt's made of cat shit," I said.

"We're sending you home, Mr. Friedman," said the doctor smoothly. "These two gentlemen have graciously agreed to take turns being your primary care-givers. If you cooperate with them, you will be fine. But there are two conditions under which I am discharging you: Number one is that you must not under any circumstances exert yourself; number two is that you are to be confined to your quarters for a period of approximately six weeks."

"Don't worry, Kinkstah!" said Ratso. "The time will fly by."

"I really must emphasize," said Skinnipipi, "that you remain in your flat until the *Plasmodium falciparum* has entirely departed your system."

"You can do it, Kink!" put in McGovern. "And we'll be there to help you."

I looked up at two big white faces and one skinny brown one. Like martinets, they turned briefly sideways to each other, then all three gazed back down at me hopefully.

"Do I have your word, Mr. Friedman?" intoned the doctor.

"Spike Lee's made of cat shit," I said.

CHAPTER SEVEN

No horsepital in America will let a patient leave the building on his own steam, which was just as well because I doubt if I could've made it. The vehicle of choice, of course, is the wheelchair, which gives you an opportunity to find out what it's like to be The Invisible Man. Outside of the few nurses and professionals who deal with this sort of thing every day, almost everyone else you meet instinctively prefers to talk to you—if they talk to you at all—through the mouthpiece of the more ambulatory person who's pushing the chair. Inside the horsepital, the wheelchair-bound virtually don't exist because they are such a common commodity. It's almost like seeing somebody pushing around a sack of potatoes. This is as it should be. The guys who put accident victims in the meat-wagon usually don't say, "Oh, God! Look at all the blood!" More likely, once the situation's under control, they'll be talking baseball or football, or, if they happen to be homosexuals, they'll be talking about Celine Dion's new CD. Likewise, a horsepital orderly is not likely to say: "Look at the poor man in the wheelchair. I wonder what's wrong with him?" They see this shit all the time. In fact, if you're not careful, in a horsepital you can get your ass run over by a wheelchair.

But when dealing with the tourists, the visitors, the families, and the wide world outside the horsepital, you rapidly find yourself transmogrified from a familiar commodity whom everyone ignores to an oddity whom everyone ignores. In other words, being wheelchair-bound means that everyone relates to you as if you were a dog or cat or infant, and it's not so bad once you get used to it. People ask the person pushing the chair, in this case McGovern, "How's he doing?" or "What happened to him?" or "Did you notice that his nose is falling off?" It takes a brave soul to talk directly to somebody in a wheelchair, and in the rare event that it happens, it's usually accomplished in nauseatingly patronizing tones. "Did we get some good rest at the hospital?" or, once they've spoken a bit to McGovern, "Are we going to follow the doctor's orders?" My response to any and all questions like this was uniformly the same: "Piss off, mate." It worked remarkably well. Even young, inquisitive children seemed to almost viscerally understand where I was coming from, and I don't mean the horsepital.

McGovern, for his part, seemed to enjoy pushing the wheelchair and answering questions for me. McGovern, of course, was the man who once combed his hair before meeting a racehorse. He was also the man who, several years earlier, had chosen to have elective surgery at the VA hospital in New York on Yom Kippur. He would not have been my first choice in the world of people I wanted to be pushing my wheelchair, but when you're in a wheelchair, there's nothing you can do about that either. Eventually, inevitably, you come to hate the person pushing your wheelchair. Even a big, kind-hearted, devoted McGovern-type will begin to get up your sleeve by the time you've rolled your pathetic way down a few of life's long, crowded, smelly corridors. The person pushing the chair can never know what it's like until he's rolled a mile on your wheels. That's why he's so friendly and fucking cheerful all the time. It makes you want to kill him, or at least hurt him enough to put him in the horsepital so he can see what it's like to be in this stupid fucking wheelchair with some high-minded asshole who probably thinks he's saving the world pushing you down the fucking street. Most people in wheelchairs are, I believe, pretty much thinking thoughts along these lines. Fortunately, they're in wheelchairs, so they can't hurt us. It's when they get better and become ambulatory again that the rest of us pedestrians have to be careful. Happily, by then they've usually forgotten their bitter, twisted, vengeful wheelchair thoughts, and they go about their normal activities, which are often composed of cheerfully pushing the rest of us around in wheelchairs. People who are permanently confined to wheelchairs are a still more dangerous animal, of course. They resent you for your ambulatory abilities which you take totally for granted and they would definitely kill you in a heartbeat if their physical impairments didn't preclude them from doing so. They've had a lot of time to think about it, time to stew in their own juices, so to speak, and if given the slightest opportunity, with or without provocation, they will attempt to trick you, or trip you, or poison you, or kill you by some extremely well-thought-out and viciously nefarious means, such as unscrewing the rotor on your new Sharper Image nose-hair clipper.

"How in the hell am I supposed to hail a taxi at the same time I'm pushing this wheelchair?" said McGovern in a tone of deep frustration.

"Tom Hanks is made of cat shit," I said.

"That's enough of that cat shit shit," said McGovern rather peevishly. "You're not delirious anymore. It's just an attention-getting device. You're doing this to irritate people."

"What's wrong with that?" I asked rationally.

"Nothing," said McGovern, "except in this case the people you're irritating is me and I'm pushing the fucking wheelchair and you're pushing me to the point where I just might push it into the goddamn street!"

"C'mon, McGovern, you don't have to feel this way. Go to the happy place."

"Fuck you and the wheelchair you rode in on," said McGovern.

While McGovern and I were dealing with our logistical and interpersonal problems, Ratso, who might have provided a fairly adequate buffer, was nowhere in sight. I soon was to learn that he'd taken the key to the loft and headed down to Big Wong's in Chinatown where he'd stocked up on approximately six weeks' worth of takeout Chinese food. I like Big Wong's almost as much as Ratso, but I thought this to be somewhat excessive, especially when I realized that he'd billed all of it to me. But I'm getting a little bit ahead of myself in my wheelchair here.

McGovern and I were now seriously involved in the business of finding a taxi. Taxis are plentiful in New York. If, indeed, you're crazy enough to drive a vehicle in the city, you've probably noticed yellowish scratches and indentations on the car's finish which we often refer to as "taxi juice." There are times when you can see whole fleets of yellow taxicabs moving inexorably down the avenues like Panzers into Poland. There are only two occasions when it's impossible to find a cab in New York: when it's raining and when you're in a wheelchair.

"Shit," said McGovern. "It's starting to rain."

CHAPTER EIGHT

I won't go into the tedium, ennui, and pure hell we experienced, first merely finding a cab, and then trying to fit a large Irishman, a malaria patient, and a collapsible wheelchair that wouldn't collapse all into a tiny yellow cab that was driven by a man whose appearance and behavior bore an almost uncanny resemblance to that of Robert Mugabe. Somehow, we managed. But arriving at 199B Vandam Street, apparently, was only to be the beginning of our problems.

"We'll never get that wheelchair up four flights of stairs," said McGovern. "What about using that old freight elevator in your building?"

"That hasn't worked in years," I said, opening the door and almost falling out of the cab.

"Neither have you," said McGovern lightheartedly.

He laughed his loud, infectious Irish laugh, which was always most effective when there wasn't really anything to laugh about. That was a pretty good description of the current situation. The driver had driven off in a snit, the wheelchair was lying in the gutter looking for all the world like a large collapsed Bohemian accordion, and we didn't have a key to the building because Ratso had taken it when he went to Big Wong's. At the moment he was probably shoveling down a large meal up there in my loft, totally oblivious to McGovern's persistent shouts for him to throw down the puppethead. The little wooden puppethead, of course, held the key to the building in its perpetually smiling mouth. The key to happiness, I'd noticed, could almost never be found in anybody's perpetually smiling mouth. At this juncture, however, I'd have been happy to settle for the key to the building.

"It's not true that I've never worked," I said to McGovern. "I've just never held a real job."

"What?" said McGovern. "Say again? Bob?"

"That's right. Bob. Bob Dylan's coming over to help us get the wheelchair up the stairs."

"I heard you," said McGovern petulantly.

Maybe it was just the ying and yang of the everyday world, but as McGovern's hearing seemed to fall into periods of inefficiency, so my fever seemed to rise and with it I quite naturally rose into heights of delirium. So we had a deaf man trying to communicate with a delusional man regarding getting into a building in which at this very moment a man with large Jewish buttocks was probably sitting on the davenport eating the cheeks—and they are regarded as delicacies—out of a large, braised fish head.

"Let's go with plan B," I said.

"Good as can be!" said McGovern, giving me the thumbs up.

"Plan B!" I shouted. "We get help to get us in the building from a passing lesbian."

"What? Say again? Thespian? There's a new play coming to town?"

"There's always a new play coming to town, McGovern," I said angrily. "We live in New York."

"I know that," he shouted. "You don't have to bite my head off! You don't have to talk to me like I'm a child!"

While very little light was produced by this particular tension convention, enough heat was generated apparently to attract the ear of one Larry "Ratso" Sloman, who promptly threw open my fourth-floor kitchen window and shouted down: "It's about time! I was getting worried about you guys."

"He's worried about getting *flies?*" asked McGovern.

"That's right," I said, feeling a swoon coming on. "The loft's probably about knee-deep by now in cat shit."

"Don't start that cat shit shit again! I'll tell Dr. Pickaninny."

"That's Dr. Skinnipipi," I said.

"Same to you," said McGovern.

During this last bleak effort at social intercourse, Ratso had thrown down the puppethead with the key in its mouth, and it now sailed like a schooner, its American flag parachute billowing beautifully over the garbage trucks, garbage cans, miscellaneous detritus, and, well—cat shit—that were endemic to Vandam Street. McGovern caught up with the puppethead just as it grazed the cab of a slow-moving garbage truck. The driver of the garbage truck was mildly amused at seeing such a large Irishman in hot pursuit of such a small puppethead, but the incident did not deter him from his duties. When you drive a garbage truck in New York, sooner or later you see everything. I remember back in Texas people often used to ask my old friend Slim, who was bugled to Jesus long before the term "African-American" was invented, why his cats always got into their garbage cans. Slim invariably gave them the same answer: "They wants to see the world."

McGovern got the key and opened the front door of the building, then Ratso came down the stairs to help walk me up to the loft. With an arm around each of their shoulders, I slowly, painfully, made it up all four flights, a journey I never would have accomplished on my own steam. God bless the Village Irregulars, I thought. On the one arm I had the niggardly, slovenly, ever loyal Ratso. On the other I had the irritating gentile optimism of McGovern. They were two towers of strength for me then, in many ways like the two no longer there, consigned for always and ever to the hearts of anyone who calls himself New Yorker. God bless the Village Irregulars, I thought. All the millions of them.

CHAPTER NINE

As I had feared, the sights and smells and sounds that greeted us as we entered the loft were not pleasant. Ratso had run ahead of McGovern and myself as we'd reached the fourth landing just to, as he said, "straighten up a bit." Even in my fevered, delirious state I could easily see that Ratso was himself either very deeply deluded or he was greatly exaggerating his ability to put lipstick on the pig. Before I could even see past McGovern's large body, I could hear that all was not well.

"Get away! Get away!" screamed Ratso. "Get away, you noxious vapor!"

The cat howled and scurried somewhere deeper into the bowels of the loft. An angry, out-of-breath Ratso appeared almost magically in the doorway.

"Your fucking cat just vomited in my new fucking backpack!" he shouted in exasperated rage.

I didn't need this. I was swaying on my feet as it was and I'd forgotten or repressed the rather ugly, acrimonious relationship that had long existed between Ratso and the cat. For reasons beyond mortal ken, the cat had always resented and despised Ratso. Ratso did not handle this situation particularly well, and his venomous outbursts invariably only served, if possible, to further irritate the cat. Animals may not understand the words you say to them, but they instinctively understand the tone, and they never forget. They also know a snitch when they see one. Over the years I'd done my best not to pick sides between Ratso and the cat, and now, it seemed, in my weakened state, I was about to reap an almost biblical harvest of hatred. Since the cat was nowhere in sight, I clung to the base of the espresso machine for support and tried to reason with Ratso.

"When a cat vomits in your backpack," I began patiently, "it is rarely an indication of malice or rancor on the part of the animal. It merely means that the cat is sick or nervous or distressed by circumstances beyond her control, which I'm certain merit the empathy and understanding of everyone in this room."

"What happened to the bottle of Jameson's?" said McGovern, rummaging wildly through the cupboard.

"The cat," said Ratso, barely concealing the note of triumph in his voice, "deliberately knocked over the bottle and it broke."

"What?" shouted McGovern. "Say again? We're out of coke?"

"Now, had the cat," I continued, "taken a Nixon in your backpack—"

46

"The cat shit in my red antique shoe when I stayed here before!"

"Yes, yes, Watson," I said, feeling feverish as Sherlock on a 7 percent solution. "The shoe in question once having belonged to a dead man, as I recall."

"His whole wardrobe once belonged to dead people," said McGovern, demonstrating once more a degree of selective hearing.

"Be that as it may," I said, "if the cat had shit in Ratso's backpack, a personal vendetta might have been in play, but vomiting hardly ever can be construed a spiteful act. Let it go, my dear Watson. It's cat piss under the bridge, as we used to say at the old Diogenes Club."

"Look, Kinkstah," said Ratso, "Dr. Skinnipipi made it quite clear that you're not to exert yourself. He says that bed rest is the only—"

"Fuck Dr. Skinnipipi and the stethoscope he rode in on," I said. "Turn on the lights, will you?"

"They're already on, Kinkstah," said Ratso. "And now I think it's time for you to get some rest. Come on, Kinkstah. Let us help you to the bedroom."

As both red phones on either side of my desk began violently clamoring, Ratso and McGovern assisted my journey to the bedroom. Without their help, I believe it surely would have been impossible. When we reached the doorway, I almost collapsed. I'd apparently underestimated just how very weak I was. I was so weak, indeed, that I forgot the instinctive Jewish reaction to always answer a telephone no matter what else I was doing at the time.

The only blight on the horizon, I now saw, was a fairly dry-looking cat turd perfectly centered upon my pillow. This rather unsavory vision stopped the three of us in our tracks and gave us, as it were, food for thought.

"Looks like the cat's an equal opportunity defecator," said Ratso, with grim disapproval in his tone.

"It's about time they fixed the elevator," responded McGovern. "It's hell always having to walk up four flights."

Ratso winked at me broadly, removed the offending pillowcase, and went in search of a fresh one. Even a person in my condition, or possibly especially a person in my condition, is aware of the importance of the little things in life. A cat turd perfectly positioned on a pillow, I suppose, is not often regarded as very important in the general scheme of the world. It does, however, undeniably indicate that somewhere, somehow, some way, someone misses you.

CHAPTER TEN

I had a lot of time on my hands and I was not afraid to use it. Unfortunately, the only thing I could use most of it for was sleeping, but I have long ago determined that sleeping may be one of the best uses of time any of us ever find during our brief sublet on this planet. Hours went by, days, weeks, possibly years. I was not well. Merely being discharged from a horsepital does not guarantee health and happiness. Quite the contrary, in fact. I still had all manner of sensory delusions. When the phones rang, for instance, which seemed to occur just about every three minutes, the whole loft appeared to become engulfed with the vibrations of a giant oriental gong. I had no idea, of course, who was calling, why they were calling, or if they were ever answered. I was too busy sleeping to be bothered much by external details. Indeed, it is quite true that often I was totally unable to discern whether or not I was truly sleeping, or possibly dreaming, or merely experiencing what, in a healthier, more normal state, I might have blithely called reality.

Reality. I recalled in lucid flashes what an old British ex-pat once told me when I was in the Peace Corps in the jungles of Borneo. He'd experienced a long and lingering case of malaria, a disease that seemed as foreign to me then as eating monkey brains, a delicacy I was soon to acquiesce to, so as not to be rude to my hosts, a nomadic tribe of pygmies called the Punans. Now I was experiencing malaria myself, albeit many years after my return from the jungle, and, amidst fever and shaking chills, I was trying desperately to remember exactly what the Brit had told me regarding malaria and reality. I could hear his voice, or maybe it was just Ratso speaking slowly, articulating each syllable with a thick British accent. What had the Brit said to me so many years ago as we sat beside a coffee-colored river near the little town of Long Lama? I had it for a moment, then I lost it, then I grasped it desperately with the gnarled fingers of my mind and I knew I'd gotten it right. "Malaria," the Brit had said, "is the only way one can see the world as it really is."

And I saw it, all right. A ghastly procession of friends passing by my bedside like half-human phantoms in a dream. Were they real? Was anything real? Were they Kayan witches in wooden canoes called *prahus* rowing up the Baram River like a deadly tidal bore where the water level rises suddenly and sweeps away everything in its path? Witches had ahold of me now with their icy fingers, and I pulled the great purple comforter up over my head and still I felt a great wave of shaking chills and the loft was filled with ice and evil and I could see that their hair was all Medusalike and their eyes were those of wild animals in the deepest *ulu* looking past my dreams to the place I would drop off the *ruai* of the world and die. And the witches smile their cold, crooked little smiles as if they knew all the while that your heart would shiver and break like a frozen shadow falling into the eternal emptiness of the sun-dappled *ulu*. And the witches' ears stretch down, past their heads and faces, pulled down by many hoops of ornamental iron, and the ears begin to flap, and the witches drop their oars and begin to fly right out of their *prahus,* right out of their coffee-colored river, and they fly into your mouth and nostrils and ears and anus and up the little hole at the business end of your pee-pee, and they bore into your soul and you realize at the end of your struggle that every witch is a shiver and every shiver is a witch.

"Well, fuck me dead, mate!"

Clear as a bell I heard the familiar Australian accent flowing across my ravaged body and sweat-soaked sheets like balm from a gum tree on a warm night under the Southern Cross. The loud stentorian voice could only belong to one human being on the entire planet, and that was impossible. My old friend Piers Aker-man should've been ten thousand miles away in Sydney. Was I just dead or just dreaming? What was he doing right here in my bed-room?

"Piers!" I shouted deliriously. "What the hell are you doing here?"

"Drinking, of course, mate."

I looked over and I saw that Piers was not speaking idly. In his hands were a bottle of Jameson's Irish Whiskey and two glasses, which he promptly filled, placing one into my trembling hand and the other to his large, smiling lips. He drained the glass, belched with satisfaction, and poured himself another hefty shot.

"I don't like to say anything, mate," said Piers, "but who's in charge of this operation? Your primary care-giver, as I understood from Brennan, is McGovern, and he appears to be passed out on your living room floor."

"How'd you get in?" I asked, the Jameson's already seeming to have a positive medicinal effect upon my malady. "What are you doing in New York?"

"Actually, I was in Colorado on a top secret mission for Rupert Murdoch when I got a message from Brennan that you were gravely ill. Are you, mate?"

"How the hell should I know? I've got malaria, I've been confined to the loft on the doctor's orders, and I've been dreaming of witches."

"And McGovern's your primary care-giver. I fed the cat, by the way. She seems to have deposited a large Nixon upon somebody's backpack. It's within the realm of possibility, of course, that McGovern himself was the Nixon depositor, but it appears most likely that it was the cat. Who does the backpack belong to?"

"Ratso. He said he was going to play hockey."

"It's two o'clock in the morning, mate."

"That's when he plays hockey. There's nothing anyone can do about it. It's the way of his people."

"Look, mate," said Piers, with a worried expression on his face. He didn't say anything else for a moment or two and it gave me just time enough to realize that I'd never seen Piers with a worried expression on his face. In my life, he was the first person I'd ever heard say, "No worries, mate." He could be abrasive, domineering, and, as a woman in Perth once told me at a cocktail party: "I find Piers Akerman quite tiresome." But he was also brilliant, loyal, kind, and extremely funny. Now, he just looked plain worried. And this, of course, had me rather worried as well.

"Ah, look, mate," said Piers again, "I'll just get my things from the hotel and camp out here with you for a few days. With McGovern, Brennan, and Ratso looking after you, I reckon the situation might require a spot of outside help. The Village Irregulars, I'm afraid, are once again demonstrating their innate abilities to be, for want of a better word, irregular."

After Piers had left to collect his stuff from the hotel, I found myself feeling surprisingly better and I left my bed for my first unaccompanied trip to the dumper. I had to step over McGovern, who, as Piers had averred, was snoring away on the floor of the living room. The cat followed me to the dumper just to be sure I could make it on my own. It felt good to know that Piers would be "camping out" at the loft. As much as I loved McGovern, Ratso, and Brennan, I wasn't sure that I really wanted to trust that terrible trio with my life. Coming back to the bedroom after a successful urinary effort, the cat following faithfully behind, I began to have my first doubts about what might possibly lie ahead. I did not like the feeling of being almost totally dependent upon others. I knew also that Piers was a party animal practically at the McGovern level himself. I could imagine some interesting times ahead. But never in my wildest dreams could I have anticipated what was about to occur in my loft and in my life.

"Well," I said to the cat, as I got back under the comforter, "I suppose a little company isn't going to hurt us."

The trip to the dumper had weakened me considerably, but I was able to gaze down and observe the cat sitting stoically on the foot of the bed. She was looking at me with pity in her eyes. "Poor human beings," she seemed to say. "They never do quite get it right."

CHAPTER ELEVEN

One of the interesting things about an illness like malaria, in which you float from altered state to altered state, is that you never know if something that has just happened is really something that has just happened. As the fever overtook me again, I found myself deeply troubled by the practical unlikelihood of Piers's visit. I wondered if my old friend from down under had actually been in my loft at all. The only witness other than the cat, of course, was McGovern, and he didn't seem to be revealing too many cards at the moment. I would, apparently, be forced to wait to see if Piers returned, no doubt carrying a large tucker bag and many bottles of grog. Or maybe, even now, he was peacefully sailing on a yacht somewhere off the Great Barrier Reef. Maybe he hadn't really been in my bedroom at all.

These are the kinds of thoughts that will drive a sane man crazy and sometimes cause a crazy man to see a world that even a sailor never gets the chance to see. It is a world of the mind, a world of the restless, troubled spirit, a world every bit as real as any other that man has yet been able to invent. It is there for the asking, in fact. All you have to do is acquire a severe case of lurid, lingering, lonely malaria. Fevered thoughts of any manner can be interrupted, however, when a large, half-Irish, half-Indian, drunk and incoherent journalist comes reeling in the most dangerous and disoriented fashion into one's little sickroom screaming at the top of his lungs.

"I had a dream!" shouted McGovern. The cat bolted for the living room and the relative safety of the davenport.

"Kayan witches?" I inquired, shivering at the thought.

"Say again?" said McGovern, leaning forward and almost falling on top of me. "Lyin' bitches?"

"Forget it, McGovern," I said, losing all patience with him. "What the hell did you have a dream about? Did you dream of Jeannie with the light tan folks? Did you dream you saw Joe Hill last night? Did you dream of little white children and little black children playing together?"

"You don't have to make fun of me," said McGovern with growing belligerence. "My dreams are just as important as anybody else's."

"Fine. So what the hell did you dream about?"

"I dreamed a large kangaroo came hopping into the loft."

"That's not so far off the mark," I said.

"Say again?" said McGovern. "You dreamed of Lewis and Clark?"

"That's right, McGovern. I dreamed of Lewis and Clark. It

means I'm going to take a trip soon. Unfortunately, I can't leave this fucking loft."

McGovern seemed to mull this information over studiously for a moment or two, then removed his large presence from the bedroom for a while, only to return some time later bearing a tray of hot coffee and a sympathetic aura, which, of course, made me feel guilty for being so acerbic with him. McGovern was a loyal and devoted friend, and I wondered, if the situation had been reversed, if I would have been as attentive to his needs as he was being to mine. Probably I would not have had the time. I'd have had to hire a large Bulgarian masseuse to take care of him. Ah, well, I thought, friendship is manifested in many different ways and sometimes it isn't manifested at all.

I was beginning to understand that malaria, like love, is one of the true deceivers in life. One moment you feel almost human and the very next, you feel you're at death's door and you wish the bastards would let you in. Dreams are real and reality's a dream. Day is night and night is day. And Einstein's Theory, of course, applies to victims of malaria: Time is relative and it goes faster if you don't have any visits from your relatives. Fortunately, I come from a small, ill-tempered family and I have very few relatives and they all live far away in Lower Baboon's Asshole. If I have a family, I suppose it is the Village Irregulars and with God shining her countenance upon us, somehow we've gotten by. So far.

But where was I before I began hearing voices in my head? Oh, yes. Piers Akerman, one of the most reliable friends I had, did not return that night as he'd indicated he would. This led me into a state of mild panic because I had now begun to believe that he'd never actually been there at all. I guess the thing to have done would have been to have called Piers in Australia to determine if his recent visit had indeed occurred or if his seemingly robust appearance was merely another dreaded chimera of my fevered, disintegrating, and sometimes rather unsavory sensibilities.

If I'd lost one Piers, however, I'd apparently gained a Ratso and a Brennan. I woke up from a highly repellent dream, which featured Kafka being bull-fucked by a kangaroo, to hear Ratso and Brennan engaged in an equally unpleasant manner of intercourse. They were in the other room, but the cat and I could hear their conversation quite clearly.

"I don't want the poor sod to croak on my watch, mate! He should be back in hospital!"

"Bullshit! Why do you think the doctor discharged him?"

"Because the sawbones is a poncey dothead! He's a tosser!"

"And you're a fucking idiot! Malaria is rarely fatal—"

"Have you looked at him lately, mate? If you'd put away your hockey stick long enough maybe you'd notice that he looks whiter than his sheets! His mind is almost completely gone! He thinks Piers Akerman was here last night!"

"I don't care if he thinks Father Damien was here last night! That's what he's supposed to think! He has malaria!"

"Bollocks! He's losin' light, I tell you. He's going downhill fast, mate. He should be back in hospital! It's on your head if he croaks!"

"He's not going to croak! McGovern was here all night!"

"Oh, McGovern's Florence Nightingale, is he? I wouldn't trust that dodgy bloke to watch a scone rise!"

"And maybe Piers Akerman was here last night."

"Not likely, mate. He's 15,989 kilometers away—"

"You Brits are all the same. Why can't you just give it to me in miles?"

"I'm not a Brit, mate. I'm just a lucky Irish lad who happened to be born in jolly old England."

"If I'd been there at the time I would've checked your father's dick with my hockey stick and stopped the inception. Don't create unnecessary trouble here. Everything's under control."

At that precise moment, a great tumult ensued upon the land. From my dank little bedroom, it sounded very much like the barbarians were at the gate. Moments later, I realized that, indeed, they were.

"Mother of God!" shouted Ratso. "Look down on the sidewalk!"

"Sweet leapin' Jesus!" shouted Brennan.

Screams and shrieks of an altogether unearthly nature could clearly be heard from the street. The sound of a windowpane smashing filled the cat and me with anxiety. We cringed in our little back bedroom, torn between mortal fear and feline curiosity.

"Do we throw them down the puppethead?" asked Ratso.

"Might as well, mate," said Mick Brennan. "When Piers Akerman and Mike McGovern get this heavily monstered, the entire Polish Army couldn't stand in their way."

CHAPTER TWELVE

For the next several days a Mardi Gras–like atmosphere seemed to reign in the loft at 199B Vandam Street. Some of the lesbians from Winnie Katz's dance class on the floor above even dropped in to join the festivities. You might think this rather outrageous behavior might not be in the better interests of a malaria patient, but you'd be wrong. Actually, it was just what the doctor ordered. For a while, at least, it lifted me out of my fevered and melancholy state and put me into very high spirits indeed. I wasn't over the malaria. Even I understood that. But, just possibly, I was over feeling sorry for myself. And that, gentile reader, is a giant step for any man to take.

The cat, to be sure, was not as understanding. Cats never are. She longed for the days when I'd sit at my desk, cobwebs attaching themselves from cigar to my cowboy hat, waiting for a case to materialize. I could hardly remember these days myself. Solving a crime, staking out a building with Rambam, pounding the pavement in search of bad guys, pounding my penis in an effort at self-gratification—all these were now things of the past. Fighting crime was the furthest thing from my mind. I was currently fighting merely to retain what was left of my mind and to survive this stubborn and unforgiving malady. It was rather fortunate, indeed, that no investigation had recently come my way. I wouldn't have had a clue how to deal with it.

Not only did the cat despise the party-making atmosphere that now often perpetrated itself upon the formerly peaceful confines of the loft, the loft itself looked like it'd taken a direct hit from a daisy-cutter. Beer cans and liquor bottles and plates containing half-eaten dinners were strewn all over the place. Mick Brennan kept promising he'd clean everything up, but so far very little progress appeared to have been made. To add to the clutter, the cat, perhaps understandably, had returned to her previous format of vindictively dumping upon practically every clean surface that my care-providers had somehow managed to miss. The result of all this was not a pleasant one to observe, much less to live amongst, but somehow the human spirit triumphed and we all managed. I managed to periodically even forget that I was a spiritual shut-in. I got out of bed fairly often now, puttered about the loft, looked for something or someone to do, found nothing, and often as not, returned to my bed in a surprisingly weakened state.

Malaria is a whore. Malaria is a tar baby. It is a noxious house-pest, one of many, I might add, who stays and stays and stays.

After periods of feeling relatively normal, I would suddenly find the fever and the shaking chills returning with a vengeance, demolishing my temporary good spirits, turning my world upside-down once again. I was, in general, certainly not myself. As Piers Akerman, I believe, observed: "The fact that the Kinkster is not himself is a silver lining for everybody else." There may have been a small kernel of truth to this statement, but I've always believed friendship is overrated, just as taking a Nixon is often underrated. I also believe that no one can truly win friends and influence people; people who like you in spite of yourself will be called friends, and those are the ones upon whom you may someday have some trivial effect. People rarely, if ever, truly "influence" others. We are all too culture-bound, too much creatures of narrow habit, too influenced by "us" to ever be much influenced by "them."

At least I wasn't feeling like Kafka anymore. The world was not out to get me. It was out to get everybody and sooner or later, no doubt, it would. If I could've kept up in the drinking department with McGovern, Piers, and Brennan, I probably would've drunk myself to death, thereby at least curing the malaria. But I couldn't keep up with them. Nobody currently living in the world could. Maybe Spencer Tracy or John Wayne or Ira Hayes or Edgar Allan Poe could but they had all been bugled to Jesus, no doubt, all with a bottle in their hands. The cat, of course, hated drunken behavior in humans and, quite irrationally, she maintained her hatred of Ratso, the only care-giver who drank in moderation. Ratso was Jewish, of course, and Jews are not often alcoholics. It's simply not the way of their people. Jews may have many other obnoxious behaviors, but one of them is not drinking. The Jew is somewhat culturally deprived in this country, however, because, growing up as a child he almost never hears the three words that most Americans live by and have grown to love: "Attention Wal-Mart Shoppers!"

Late one night, while experiencing one of my more severe attacks of fever, I found myself mulling over the possibility that the cat was a Nazi. This would explain her hatred of Ratso. It would not, of course, explain why she continued to contentedly live in my loft. It was conceivable, I thought, that the cat could be a Nazi spy, fighting down her inherent anti-Semitic tendencies until her mission in America was completed. This might go a ways toward explaining her rather unsavory dumping behavior. Working against this theory, I reflected, was the indisputable fact that the cat had Jewish eyes that were, like all true Jewish eyes, sad, beautiful, and indefatigably distrustful of people. The cat as a Nazi, I had to admit, was somewhat far-fetched, but life, malaria, and—well—sometimes cats, will do that to you. In the end, as you might suspect, I didn't buy the theory. For the cat was sleeping peacefully next to me on the pillow, her head resting lovingly on my shoulder. Clearly, she loved me as much as a cat can love a man and I, for my part, loved her as much as a man can love a cat. Between the two of us, I thought, we very probably were imbued with more love than all the Nazis in the world.

But loving someone, whether or not that someone happens to be a cat, does not necessarily mean that you can sleep. Malaria can be so debilitating, can so ravage the system, that you can't sleep when you need to sleep, you can't shit when you need to shit, you can't laugh when you need to laugh, and you can't say what you need to say. It's a little bit, in fact, the way most of us live every day of our lives.

Since I couldn't sleep, I got up and began rummaging restlessly through the drawers and cabinets and closets of the loft. I didn't know what I was looking for but most people fall into that department most of their lives: the lost and never found. It helps to know what you're looking for, but it's no guarantee you'll still want it once you find it. When I began puttering about the living room I discovered that none of my supposed care-givers were anywhere in sight. Far from disturbing my fragile constitution, this unusual occurrence caused a small wave of peace to billow over my heart. I had not been alone in the loft since the whole ordeal had begun, and now I was positively luxuriating in my solitude.

To borrow a colorful Aussie expression from Piers Akerman, the loft did look rather "shithouse," but at least for the moment we now had the population explosion somewhat under control. Piers's huge appetite for food, alcohol, and life did not have to be constantly attended to. There were no sounds of bickering between Brennan and McGovern or Brennan and Ratso. All in all, the place seemed pretty peaceful. This is not to say that I was ungrateful for the care and concern of the Village Irregulars. The medical practice well understands that malaria patients, like many other patients of many other disorders, tend to overdo things when they think they're getting better. The result is invariably a discouraging and damaging relapse, placing the patient's prognosis further in jeopardy than it previously had been. This is what the members of the medical practice believe, but they are only correct about half the time. That's why the practice of medicine is called a practice.

I hadn't smoked a cigar in a long time, so I thought I'd give it a try. I wandered over to my old desk, sat down heavily in the chair, and lifted the deerstalker cap off the top of Sherlock Holmes's porcelain head. I carefully extracted one Epicure Number 2 Cuban cigar from the depths of Sherlock's cranium, lopped off the butt with a silver butt-cutter given to me by Billy Joe Shaver on our most recent musical tour of Australia, and set fire to it with a kitchen match. The cat, who was now positioned on the desk perfectly equidistant between my two red telephones, watched with quiet encouragement. To her it seemed as if I were getting back to normal. To me, the two little Statue of Liberty torches that I saw reflected in the eyes of the cat reminded me of the wistful freedom I currently did not enjoy. I puffed peacefully on the cigar for a time and wished fervently that I could be my old self again. But deep in my soul I felt as ephemeral and insubstantial as the blue-gray smoke of my cigar, dissipating slowly into the lesbian sky. If my faculties, both physical and spiritual, did not return to me soon, I would not survive my confinement in this loft. Claustrophobia, not malaria, would eventually do me in.

"Will the game ever be afoot again?" I said to the plaster saint, the ceramic muse, the whatever-the-hell-he-was-made-of god that was Sherlock Holmes.

He did not answer. This was good. Maybe I was getting better.

"I hate to say it," I said to the cat, "but I'm almost ready to tackle an investigation."

The cat was conducting her own investigation at the moment. She was investigating her anus. Possibly, she was just trying to get the taste out of her mouth after sampling some of the plates of left-

66

over food lying about. At any rate, she did not understand that smoking the cigar, at least momentarily, put me in touch with myself, brought me to my senses, made me realize that my life was nothing without a mystery.

Maybe this was why I soon found myself standing at the kitchen window, scanning the narrow horizons of Vandam Street, looking through a pair of old, not to say archaic, opera glasses. This museum relic had been given to me by my old friend, Aunt Anita. Aunt Anita had a little dog named Ipo, which means "sweetheart" in Hawaiian. Both Aunt Anita and Ipo had long since gone to Jesus. Now, only I remained, looking at the world through her old opera glasses, searching, searching, for something I'd lost on yesterday street.

CHAPTER THIRTEEN

I f I hadn't have been in a state of malarial unfocusment, I probably never would have seen it in the first place. I also probably wouldn't have been standing at the kitchen window with a pair of ancient opera glasses hovering just above my beezer. But there I was. And there it was. A small square of light in a world of darkness.

"I can't believe it!" I shouted to the cat. "This little booger really works!"

The cat's interest seemed mildly piqued. At least she seemed curious enough to jump off the desk and hop up beside me on the windowsill. Coming from a cat, that's quite a vote of confidence.

The square of light was apparently an apartment or loft in the building across the street which I'd always taken to be just an old warehouse. People who looked at my building, I reflected, very possibly just took it to be an old warehouse. Yet, beneath the facades, behind the exteriors, under the waves, between the sheets, inside the hearts, where nobody looks is always where the real show is taking place. I had no idea what time it was or what day it was. All I knew was that it was dark outside and it was late and there was a small table inside the lighted square with a vase of flowers on it.

"Looks like *Still Life with Woodpecker*," I hazarded, in a rather half-hearted effort to keep the cat in the game. Mentioning a bird usually helped, but I could see that her interest was rapidly waning.

The fact is, my interest was waning, as well, until the woman came into the frame. Indeed, before I saw her, I'd gotten bored and had shifted my attention to a cat going through a parked garbage truck. You'd think my cat, who lived, relatively speaking, in the very lap of luxury, might have some little degree of empathy for the stray cat poring over the garbage. This was not the case, however. The cat saw the other cat, gave a slight mew of distaste, hopped down from the windowsill, and immediately redirected her attention to her own anus. Socially speaking, I was somewhat disappointed in the cat. Maybe there were some Freudian aspects to the situation that I was missing. I didn't want to go crazy thinking about it. Maybe a cat licking her own anus, another cat going through a garbage truck, and a vase of cut flowers in an empty apartment was all there was to life.

It was while I aimed the opera glasses one last time at the vase of flowers that I saw the woman enter the picture. She seemed to adjust the flowers slightly in the vase, then she walked over to the window and appeared to be gazing down on Vandam Street, possibly waiting for someone. She was not scantily clad or anything like that. She was wearing a dark house robe, or it could have been a kimono. Her hair was long and dark and cascaded down to her shoulders which, like the rest of her figure that I could see, seemed trim and lithe. She looked quite beautiful with her arms held together under her breasts in an attitude of wistful waitingness, almost the stoic pose of an island maiden standing on the shore, longing for her sailor to return. Maybe it was the malaria talking, but I had to tell someone what I felt for the girl, so I tried again to engage the cat.

"Look at this beautiful young woman," I said. "She's a modern-day Juliet waiting for her Romeo."

The cat never had cared much for the classics. Nor did she appear to ever evince much sympathy for the underdog. For those reasons, and probably many others, she continued to callously lick her anus.

"Stop licking your anus!" I shouted.

The cat did not stop. The woman, I noticed, had given up, for the moment, looking for her lover. She walked back to the table, sat down in a chair, and put her head in her hands, remaining frozen there in what seemed a heartbreaking tableau.

"Young love in the city," I said.

The cat evidently did not care a flea about the troubled lives of the people in the building across the street. She shamelessly continued her previous activity.

"Stop licking your anus!" I shouted.

The cat stopped briefly, then she started up again. I put down the opera glasses for a moment, puffed patiently on the cigar, and glanced down at an empty Vandam Street and the building across the way, which now stood almost entirely in darkness except for the light in the woman's loft. Her place was apparently one floor below mine and it was backlit nicely, almost like a movie set, but I still couldn't see much without the opera glasses. When I picked them up again and gave my malarial eyes a chance to focus, I saw that the girl was standing up again, gesturing with her hands in an agitated manner, seemingly arguing with someone else who'd evidently entered the room while I'd been watching the cat lick her anus. Life turns on a dime, they say.

As I watched, a dark shadow fell across the table. Then the dark figure of a man moved slowly—relentlessly, it seemed— across the room. The girl appeared to shrink away from him in fear. I could be wrong, I thought. Maybe she's just upset with him for being late. Very possibly the same scenario was being enacted at that moment in a great many residences all across the city. I had no idea what time it was, of course. I had no way of knowing how late the guy was. I thought maybe he'd stop and they'd stand their ground and argue some more, but that didn't happen. What happened was he kept moving toward her with an almost menacing grace, moving like nothing could stop him, like a maestro taking the stage to conduct a personal symphony of hate. For there was definitely hate and impending violence in that room and it traveled through the little opera glasses right down to my shivering bones. Sometimes malaria makes you shiver and sometimes it's only life.

He hit her then, hard, in the face and her head snapped back and her hair flowed and billowed like in a TV shampoo commercial or a movie which this wasn't and the cat stopped licking her anus and I felt like someone had hit me, too, and there wasn't a fucking thing I could do about it.

"Jesus Christ!" I shouted and the guy hit her again and Jesus Christ looked sadly down from some little hill or other and there wasn't a fucking thing he could do either. It was just a small aspect of the human condition called domestic violence and the society was redolent of it and the whole world reeked of it and maybe Hank Williams was right and they did have a license to fight, but the night was cold and the windows were all down and it made no sound and that made the normal shitty human thing all the more horrible and unearthly. And he hit her again and I turned and ran to call 911 and I stepped on an empty bottle and I fell and I was down and I crawled back to the window and I grabbed the little opera glasses and I looked across the blameless night and she was down, too, and he hit her again and again and again and only me and the cat and Jesus could see and it made us all feel sad and lonely, but we keep hoping and we keep trying and we crawl to the desk and grab the blower and we call 911 and we tell the lady who is there who we are and where we are and why we are lonely and why we are sad.

Chapter Fourteen

Okay, where's the guy who called 911?"

"Right there, officer. You all right, Kinkstah?"

"The guy on the floor? He called 911?"

"You okay, Kink?"

"Of course he's not okay. You bastards all left and you told me you'd watch him."

"When we left he was fine. He was sleeping. You said you'd be back sooner."

"Mr. Friedman, can you hear me? Did you call 911?"

"He's going to be okay. He's just weak. He's recuperating."

"I'd be recuperating, too, if I was responsible for all these empty bottles."

"He didn't drink 'em. They did!"

"So arrest me. It's legal, innit? Prohibition's over, innit?"

"I'll just tidy up now."

"Don't touch those empty bottles. What's his given name?"

"Kinky. He has a few other given names but that should suffice for your purposes."

"Kinky? What kind of name's Kinky?"

"You don't know who that is? That's Kinky Friedman. He's solved more mysteries than anybody else in New York!"

"Right!"

"Can he leap tall buildings?"

"Look, officers, there's obviously been some mistake here. Mr. Friedman's been under great strain and duress lately but it's all normal and it's all associated with the long and painful recovery period from malaria."

"That's right. He's not himself."

"He sure looks like himself. He seems to be coming around. Let's ask him if he's himself."

"Mr. Friedman? Are you the party who called 911?"

"I'm sure there's some mistake, officer."

"The mistake was you guys leaving him here alone."

"He was sleeping peacefully in his bed, mate. It's legal to let a bloke sleep in peace, innit?"

"Bullshit!"

"Bollocks!"

"You're an asshole."

"You're a poofter."

"Asshole *not* from El Paso!"

"My heroes have always been faggots."

"That's enough! We'll take you all down to the precinct."

"No, wait! He's opening his eyes!"

I felt like a guy who'd been hit by a car in the streets of Manhattan. There was a circle of faces all around me, all slowly coming into focus, all looking very concerned. I'd been hearing every word for some time now, but I just hadn't had the strength to open my eyes. Now I saw that Ratso, Brennan, McGovern, and Akerman were all there, with McGovern giving me a tentative thumbs-up sign that I didn't really understand. There were also two faces I'd never seen before. They belonged, apparently, to two cops, a tall, thin white man and a short, chubby black woman. My four friends were smiling. The two cops were not.

"Did you call 911, Mr. Friedman?" asked the tall, thin, male cop.

I was sitting up on the floor now with Piers helping to support me. The 911 call seemed like a lifetime ago. I couldn't seem to think coherently.

"Did you call 911, Mr. Friedman?" the short, chubby, black female cop demanded.

"Yes," I said weakly.

"And you called to report what?" asked the other cop.

Images and words were now forming in my jumbled, fevered brain, but I was having a hard time sorting them out. I knew something terrible had happened. I just wasn't sure what it was.

"Why did you call 911, sir?" asked the female cop relentlessly.

"Because tiny men with large penises were coming up the fire escape?"

"Sounds like Brennan," said Ratso.

"Sod off," said Brennan.

"He may have had a concussion," said the female cop.

"There's a bird on my back," I said.

"Maybe Mr. Friedman needs to come in for a psychiatric examination," said the male cop.

"He'll be fine," said Piers. "He's merely experiencing a malarial relapse. Quite common in the tropics, actually."

"Are you a doctor, sir?" the female cop asked Piers rather pointedly.

"I have lived amongst the aboriginals," said Piers, who was obviously very drunk, "and I have witnessed a great many extremely graphic ceremonial and anatomical events, some of which I'm not at liberty to divulge. I have seen the songman point the bone at a rather hapless fellow who, of course, died a horrible death within forty-eight hours. They invariably do. I have witnessed the corkscrew-shaped penis of the redback spider which can kill a man within forty-eight seconds, usually after having been bitten on the buttocks while defecating in an outdoor loo. I have observed that the magpie has, proportionally, the largest testicles in the avian kingdom."

Nobody was listening to Piers anymore, but he continued nattering on. By this time, McGovern and the male cop had gotten me to my feet and I was sitting in a chair sipping a hot tea Ratso had brought me. I was trying to remember why everybody was here when the cat jumped in my lap. Suddenly, it all began coming back to me in a cold, melancholy rush. I realized that the cops knew why I'd called 911, they just wanted to be sure that I knew why I'd called. And now, at last, it had come back to me. The cat and I both jumped up from the chair.

"I remember!" I shouted. "It's all coming back to me! The guy across the street was hurting the woman!"

The two cops were giving me encouraging nods now. I walked quickly across to the kitchen window and they followed me like two little puppies. The cat followed, too, but not like a puppy. Cats never follow like puppies. They follow only because they know that some day the opportunity may come for them to lead. The Village Irregulars stood around looking like somebody'd hit them with a hammer. They didn't know whether to shit or go bowling. You really couldn't blame them, however. They didn't know that malaria lets you see the world as it really is.

"I was standing at this window," I said to the cops. "The lights are all off now, but the last time I saw her she was down and she hadn't gotten up."

"Point to the appropriate locations where this assault took place," invited the female cop.

"Right about there," I said, pointing to where I'd seen the lighted window. "Definitely third floor. Just above where that garbage truck is parked."

"You guys stay here," said the male cop, as he and his partner headed for the door. "We're going to check this out right now."

After the cops had slammed the door, I stood at the window for a moment, watching the street. Then I relit my cigar and turned around. Everybody in the room stared at me with a look of naked curiosity in their eyes. Everyone, that is, except the cat.

CHAPTER FIFTEEN

Indubitably, the dynamics had now changed. The cops, at long last, saw me as a good citizen and a reasonably reliable witness to a crime. The Village Irregulars looked like they didn't have a clue as to what was happening. I wasn't going to tell them too fast. I picked up the cat, an act she did not especially enjoy, and took her over to my desk, and we both sat down together. It didn't take long for the proverbial shit to hit the proverbial fan. Ratso, practically salivating to play his role as Dr. Watson, was the first to head up the inquisition.

"Kinkstah!" he said. "So who's the mystery woman, Kinkstah?"

"I have malaria, Ratso. I hardly know who *you* are."

"You mean you've never seen this woman before?"

"Sometimes I don't know who I am—"

"Let me get this straight," said Piers in a loud, stentorian voice. "You witnessed something in an apartment across the street in the brief occasion all of us were gone from the loft?"

I didn't love the doubtful tone that permeated Piers's line of questioning. I wasn't feeling all that well anyway, so I didn't answer. I just decided I'd hold my breath until I popped. If the Village Irregulars didn't choose to believe me, that was their problem.

"Do you really think you witnessed a crime, Kink?" said McGovern, in a voice reserved for a foreign exchange student.

"That malaria'll play tricks on you, mate," put in Brennan.

"Oh, I get it," I said, with growing irritation. "No one believes I saw something."

"We believe you *think* you saw something," said Ratso. "In light of your condition this past week, all the fever and crazy dreams and hallucinations, not to mention your restless spirit being confined here to the loft, it's just possible that you—"

"Made it up?" I said defiantly.

"Not 'made it up,'" said Ratso. "Perhaps just *imagined* it?"

"You do have a very vivid imagination, Kink," put in McGovern, not unkindly.

"I can't believe this," I said. "I'm well aware that I'm recuperating from an illness. And I'm grateful to you guys for looking after me—"

"You're not just recuperating," put in Piers. "You've been cookin' on another planet most of the time."

"Remember *The English Patient,* mate?" said Brennan.

"Yeah," I said. "I saw the movie with my dad and it lasted about seven and a half hours. Afterward, my dad said: 'War is hell; *The*

English Patient is tedious.' What the hell's *The English Patient* got to do with anything? The guy was totally out where the buses don't run. I'm perfectly sane and sober, which is more than I can say about some of you."

"That's because you ain't the English Patient, mate," said Brennan maliciously. "You're the soddin' Jewish Patient, ain't you?"

"The Jewish Patient," laughed McGovern, with his loud Irish laugh. "That's a good one."

"Calling me names doesn't change what I saw," I said, striving for a little dignity amidst the laughter and good-natured jibes of my friends. "I saw a man practically beat a woman to death in an apartment right across the street from where I'm sitting now. I didn't see the woman get up. For all I know, the bastard might've killed her."

"You're sure they weren't practicing tai chi?" asked Piers.

"Or rehearsing for an off-off-off-Broadway play?" asked McGovern.

"Or filming a rough sex porno flick?" asked Brennan.

I didn't answer. I just stroked the cat and did my best not to stroke out with irritation. Not being believed by people who say they are your friends is always a nasty pill to swallow. It's almost as bad as watching a man try to kill a woman with his bare hands.

"Look, guys," said Ratso, seemingly coming to my rescue. "Let's suspend reality for a moment and give the Kinkstah a chance. Maybe he *did* see something."

"Of *course* I did."

"Of *course* you did," said Brennan, patting me on the back patronizingly.

"Look, mates," said Piers, "the Kinkster's been through quite a rough row as it is. Let's not rush to judgment on this matter. The cops are checking things out across the street and I'm sure they'll do a very thorough job. Then they'll come back and report what they've found to us. In the meantime, all we have to do is wait."

"Why don't we have some of this while we wait?" said McGovern, extracting a very large joint from somewhere on his very large person.

"Are you crazy?" said Ratso. "The cops'll be back here any minute."

"Don't worry, mate," said Brennan, taking the joint from McGovern and firing it up. "Kinky's cigar and the four inches of cat shit on every flat surface around here will mask any offending odors."

"That's right, mate," said Piers, taking the joint from Brennan, inhaling a superhuman hit, and passing it along to me. "The cops'll never notice. When I first walked into Kinky's flat, the cat shit combined with the stale cigar smoke was almost enough to make me gag. Have some, Kinkster. We may be waiting a long time."

I took a puff of the joint and passed it along to McGovern. Only Ratso refused to partake. Instead, he went around the loft opening a number of windows to the frigid night air.

"That cold air rushing in'll be good for somebody with the fever, mate," said Brennan.

"Not to mention," added McGovern, "that it smells worse outside where all the garbage trucks are parked."

"One of us has to keep a level head around here," said Ratso defensively. "Otherwise the cops are liable to haul all our asses in."

"Don't worry about the coppers," said Brennan. "They probably found a doughnut shop and forgot all about us. That little black treacle *looks* like a doughnut."

"That's alarmingly racist," said Ratso.

"It's also alarmingly sexist," I added.

"It's also alarmingly late," said Piers, with a yawn. "I think I'll crash for the night. I'll take the couch."

"I've got the couch," said McGovern.

"I've got the couch," said Piers. "I thought you looked quite contented on the floor the other night."

"That was because I couldn't get to the couch," protested McGovern.

"I've come halfway around the world to get to this couch, mate," Piers continued. "Why don't you let me have it?"

"Okay," said McGovern belligerently. "I'll let you have it."

With that he took a big, drunken windmill swing at Piers Akerman's head which, had it connected, no doubt would have caused the Aussie to see every star in the Southern Cross. However, the blow went wide and the result was the rather unseemly spectacle of Piers and McGovern grappling around with each other like two deranged polar bears at three o'clock in the morning in the middle of the loft. Piers, who was no small man himself, almost managed to wrestle McGovern to the floor at one point, but he slipped on a cat turd and had to confine his efforts to retaining his own balance.

"No break dancing!" shouted Brennan, pointing and laughing at Piers.

Piers was heading toward Brennan like a drunken, angry bee when a sharp series of knocks were heard by all on the door of the loft.

"Open up!" came a no-nonsense voice. "Police!"

"How'd they get back in the building without the puppethead?" I asked, not unreasonably.

"You have your methods, Sherlock," said Ratso. "They have theirs."

Ratso walked over and opened the door but the cops did not come in. Instead, they stood out in the hallway, conversing with Ratso in low tones. Occasionally, we could see Ratso nodding his head, as if in approval or understanding. After some time, Ratso closed the door and walked slowly back into the living room. On his face was an expression of something approaching sadness.

"Well," I said. "Did they check the third floor?"

"There is no third floor," said Ratso. "The third floor's just an empty warehouse. No one lives there. But they did interview all occupants, and there weren't that many apparently, on the fourth and second floors of the building. Nobody saw or heard anything."

I sensed a cold knot forming at the pit of my stomach. It felt like I was the only sane person in the world. Either that, I figured darkly, or else I was a good deal sicker than I thought I was. Either way, I was numb. I could not speak. As if in sympathy to my sensibilities, a silence prevailed in the loft for a long moment. Then, at last, Ratso spoke in the hushed, somber tones usually reserved for the dead or dying.

"Well," he said. "I guess that settles it."

"Not quite, mate," piped up Brennan. "There *is* one question."

"What's that?" asked Ratso.

"Who gets the couch?" said Brennan.

CHAPTER SIXTEEN

Things were not the same in the loft after that night. Oh, life went on, of course. Obla-dee, Obla-dah, all that shit. But a subtle human chemistry had changed between the Village Irregulars and myself, and I doubted if it would ever be the same again. Perhaps unfairly, I perceived their behavior to have become increasingly patronizing and condescending. As for myself, quite frankly, I finally understood how Jesus must have felt when he at last discovered that he'd been betrayed by Judas. In my case, of course, the injury was compounded. There were four Judases, and though at times their behavior more resembled that of the Three Stooges, their collective attitude served as a crushing blow to an already severely weakened spirit.

It was a morning several days after I'd witnessed the horrific attack that no one believed had actually occurred. The loft was populated at the moment only by McGovern, myself, and the cat. I was sitting at my desk sipping some hot Indian tea that Dr. Skin-nipipi had apparently recommended McGovern administer to the patient. The tea tasted vaguely like urine but I wasn't sure whose. It wasn't helping me. Nothing was helping me. I suppose I'd become somewhat obsessed with what I'd seen, and lately I found myself sitting at the desk, forlornly fondling the little pair of opera glasses and wondering about my sanity.

Piers was a star journalist for the *Sydney Daily Telegraph* and Brennan had major photo assignments on a fairly regular basis, so thankfully the two of them were not in attendance at the loft all the time. Ratso came and went and I did not know, nor particularly wish to know, where he was going or what he was doing. It was enough to have a temporary cessation in the seemingly eternal bickering between him and Mick Brennan, not to mention the ridiculous sumo wrestling between Piers and McGovern. Still, there are times in your life when it's a good thing not to be left totally alone and I suppose recuperating from a debilitating, delir-ium-producing illness is one of them.

McGovern was a working journalist, too, of course, but his work schedule, so he told me, was quite flexible and he rarely had to punch any time-clocks or, for that matter, editors. Now, I noticed, true to his word, he was finally getting around to cleaning up the loft. There was something rather poignant actually about the big man walking around the loft with a long-handled barbeque fork, spearing the ubiquitous dried cat turds and depositing them in the garbage bag he carried with him.

"That's very Gandhilike work you're doing," I told him. "And don't think it goes unappreciated."

"Thanks, boss," said McGovern, neatly stabbing a cat turd that had been hiding under the rocking chair. "But I don't think I'll be giving up my day job any time soon."

"According to Piers Akerman," I said, "Gandhi's system was so pure that occasionally he drank his own urine."

"You don't say."

"Piers says when those old Indian guys got on the piss, they really got on the piss. Reason I mention it is because this tea tastes like Gandhi's piss and I was just wondering if Dr. Skinnipipi revealed to you any of its ingredients."

"Come to think of it, he never told me. And no ingredients were listed on the packets."

"Probably is Gandhi's piss then."

"Well, that's certainly better than drinking Hemingway's piss or Elvis's piss."

"True. I hadn't thought of it that way."

Once again I was impressed by McGovern's apparent selective hearing. It seemed he was able to carry on a conversation perfectly until the moment I realized he was, at which point, like a dog or a horse, he'd pick up some reduced cue no human being could sense, and he'd start up his deafness routine again. Or maybe it would just kick in unconsciously. No, I thought, the bastard is doing it deliberately.

"By the way," I said, loudly and clearly, "it was nice of you to let Piers sleep on the couch."

"What?" said McGovern. "Say again? You think it appears that I'm being a grouch?"

"No, McGovern. I ground a lit cigar into my forehead and I said 'Ouch!'"

"Say again? Piers comes from a pouch?"

It had to be deliberate, I thought, as I put the opera glasses away in a desk drawer next to an old black and white photograph of a little girl holding her father's hand at an airport. Had that little girl been alive today, I believed she would have believed that I saw what I saw. But little girls don't always grow up. Some of them die when they're twenty-seven and remain little girls in black and white photographs forever, holding on to their fathers' hands. We're all little girls in photographs, if you think about it. Most of us just don't know it yet.

I was in a rather peculiar situation, I thought. It wasn't even a matter of whether or not I'd been, or indeed, was, delirious. It was more a matter of indisputable fact. Dead people seemed more willing to understand and accept what I had to say. The living, god bless 'em, just wouldn't believe me. Unless I was ready to kill everybody in the elevator, I figured, I was going to have a long, lonely ride up to the Penthouse of Truth. But I planned to fool them all. I planned to stick to my guns. Unfortunately, I didn't believe in carrying a weapon. As I sometimes pointed out to the Village Irregulars, if someone was going to kill me, he'd better remember to bring his own gun. Well, I thought with an odd sense of cheerfulness, maybe some day someone would. Then I'd know how a little girl in an old photograph feels.

CHAPTER SEVENTEEN

Suddenly the red telephones on either side of my head were ringing and I realized I must have nodded out. McGovern's large form, slumbering away on the davenport after completion of his cat turd clean-up operation, lent further confirmation to the fact that I'd been asleep. I couldn't tell how long I'd been out of it but Gandhi's piss was now stone cold. It's not a healthy thing to fall asleep while sitting at your desk. It's also not a healthy thing to listen to two red telephones ringing on either side of your head. I picked up the blower on the left.

"Start talkin'," I said.

"Kiinnnk," said a familiar voice, in a deep, familiar humorously condescending manner. It sounded almost like a frog croaking. It was Kent Perkins, my private investigator pal from L.A. Though

Kent's claim to fame was his marriage to Ruth Buzzi, he was a hell of a PI. He'd even started his own agency, Allied Management Resources, which, from everything I'd heard, had taken Los Angeles by storm.

"How's my second-favorite PI doing?" I asked.

"Who's your first?"

"Everybody else."

"Kiiinnnnnnk."

What always irritated me about the "Kiinnnk" business was that if Kent and I were arguing about something in public, all he had to do was say "Kiinnnk" a few times, quietly, as if he understood me better than I understood myself, and anyone observing would automatically assume that Kent was right and I was wrong. If I kept arguing with him, he'd just say "Kiinnk" a few more times and shake his head and they'd think I was on the very verge of insanity, which, on this particular occasion, sadly, I very possibly was.

As I explained to Kent, in some detail, the violent incident I'd witnessed, I began feeling better and better about the situation. Here at last was a real friend and, maybe more important, a true professional to tell my side of the story to. The Village Irregulars, after all, were amateurs, weekend warriors, and the gang who couldn't shoot straight. What the hell did they know? Not only that, but the cops that had taken the 911 call were merely uniforms, quite low on the NYPD food chain. This was what it was like, I thought, to be an average citizen in trouble. I knew, of course, that I wasn't an average citizen. But I was in trouble. Anybody puffing on an unlit cigar and sipping a cold cup of Gandhi's piss is definitely in trouble.

"One question," said Kent. "Why didn't you call Rambam in on this one? It sounds more like it might be his cup of tea."

I looked down at my own cup of tea but decided not to mention it to Kent. My credibility was already scraping bottom in New York, I didn't need L.A. piling on.

"I can't call Rambam," I said. "He's off somewhere in South Africa jumping through his asshole with some crack unit, no pun intended, of the South African Royal Mounted Fuckhead Paratroop Squad or whatever they're called."

"You don't seem too happy about it."

"Of course, I'm not. Rambam could get to the bottom of this. Nobody else around here believes me."

"Kiinnnnk."

"I'm telling you, goddamnit, I saw this guy with my own eyes right across the street beating the living shit out of this woman. Don't tell me *you* don't believe me. Why would I make something like this up?"

"Oh, I believe you, Kink. It just doesn't seem to quite add up. What is it you're not telling me?"

"I'm telling you the whole fucking thing. I saw the guy beat up the woman—"

"Kiinnk."

"I called 911 and the cops came and they wouldn't believe me—"

"Kiinnk."

"My dear friends the Village Irregulars don't believe me—"

"Kiinnnk."

"When the guy kills the woman next time maybe then they'll believe me."

"Why do all these people say they don't believe you? There has to be some reason."

Here is where, I knew, it could get a little dicey. In my desperate state, Kent Perkins, old friend and professional PI that he was, had now come to represent the last twisted thread of spit by which my sanity was hanging. If Kent went against me, I might as well attach a parachute to my head and shove the key to the building in my mouth and put my own head up on the mantel next to the puppethead. But that wouldn't be fair to the puppethead. He'd worked hard to get where he was, he'd had a lot of ups and downs, and now he was smiling at me, rather patronizingly, I thought, from high above the cheery fire in the fireplace. Well, I wasn't a head-hunter, I thought. I wasn't one to take another man's job. Hell, I'd often thought of him as my last true friend in New York. Now he was staring at me with pity in his eyes.

"You're not back on Peruvian marching powder, are you?" Kent was asking.

"Hell, no. I stopped snorting cocaine when a priest chased an altar boy out of my left nostril."

"That kind of talk will endear you to Catholics."

"Hey, I like Catholics. Some of my best friends are Catholics, or at least they were Catholics. And I like the pope. He always leans to the right."

"I never have a problem believing someone's tale of domestic violence. It's the ugly underbelly of the American family that no one ever sees. I ask you one more time, what haven't you told me?"

"I've been ill."

"You've been ill for almost thirty years. Why bring it up now?"

"Because the fucking doctor has confined me to my fucking loft and the Village Irregulars are now spying upon me and betraying me like Judas did to Jesus!"

"I see."

"I've got malaria. Some relapse from my days in Borneo with the Peace Corps. Can't leave the loft. Can't investigate the case myself. I have been delirious at times but, believe me, Kent, I know what I saw two nights ago. Or was it three nights ago?"

"I believe you, Kink. And I already have some ideas about this. We can go over it when I get to New York next week."

"I didn't know you were coming to New York. That's great!"

"I left you a message. At least I left it with someone at your number."

"All my little helpers," I said, quoting my father. "But this is great news, Kent. We'll blow the top off this thing!"

"If it's any comfort, Kink, you probably did witness an act of domestic violence. The problem is endemic. The statistics are on your side. And, by the way, so am I."

After I cradled the blower with Kent Perkins I felt better than I'd felt since the whole ordeal had begun. I looked the head of Sherlock Holmes right in the eye. Neither of us blinked.

"The game is afoot, brother," I said. "And this time we'll do it with or without Watson."

"Who was that who called?" shouted McGovern from the couch.

"Just a friend," I said. "Just an angel from L.A."

"Say again? What was that? The *bagels* have *decayed?*"

95

CHAPTER EIGHTEEN

The bagels, of course, had not decayed. The only thing that had decayed recently was my relationship with the Village Irregulars. Though they occasionally brought me a newspaper or a cup of hot Gandhi piss or inquired ever so sensitively about my "condition," basically I now saw them as impediments to my life. They were not only getting in the way of my investigating an act of domestic violence right here on Vandam Street, they were getting in the way of truth. They were obstructing justice, for God's sake. Or maybe they thought they were doing it for my sake. Either way, they were wrong.

Anyone who gets in the way of justice or truth is doing a disservice to God and man and must be dealt with accordingly. When I was fully recovered, I vowed, I would be making some rather drastic changes in my interpersonal relationships. Heads would roll, in fact. And I wasn't referring to smiling little wooden heads attached to parachutes.

Because the Irregulars were working against me instead of with me, I was reduced to waiting for them to depart the loft at various hours of the night and then furtively retrieving the opera glasses from the desk drawer and taking up my station by the kitchen window. I spent many a peaceful hour by that window with the cat at my side and a hot cup of Gandhi's urine or whatever the hell it was steaming on the nearby sill. Though I watched the comings and goings in other windows in the building across the street, I did not see any further activity in the loft I knew to be the scene of the crime. After a few more days had passed, indeed, I wasn't quite sure if the loft I was observing had been precisely the one in which the evil deed had taken place.

I became obsessed with the imminent arrival of Kent Perkins, whom I was convinced could effect a satisfactory resolution to the matter. As an amateur detective, as a mender of destinies, it disturbed me greatly that the situation remained unresolved. I did not share this information with the Village Irregulars, of course. I did, however, let a few tidbits drop now and then to the cat.

"I don't see a fucking thing going on in that building. Do you?"

The cat, of course, said nothing. The cat detested violence of any kind, unless the violence was being committed by herself upon some hapless creature far smaller than she was. To her, no doubt, that didn't really count as violence. It was just a game. It was merely the way of her people. It was simply good, clean, feline fun.

"You'd think we'd see something in that apartment. The very fact that we don't is singularly odd, don't you think?"

Apparently, the cat hadn't thought about it much. Nobody in the world with the exception of myself seemed to give a good goddamn that a woman was practically beaten to within an inch of her life in an apartment right under all of our noses.

"Am I here all alone?"

The cat did not answer. She rarely chose to answer questions of a rhetorical nature.

"Just wait until Perkins gets here! Then you're going to see some action. Kent will turn the whole damn Village upside-down to get that bastard! He'll grab hold of this case like a bulldog gnawing a bone. Sorry, that was an unfortunate analogy."

The cat, however, seemed to take the bulldog reference in stride. In fact, at the moment she seemed to be striding about the loft, staring intently up at the ceiling. It was almost as if she had seen something that no one else could see. Given my current circumstances, I could empathize.

"I've known Kent Perkins since long before you were even born. I met him in L.A. about thirty years ago and we discovered we were both from Texas and I'd still trust him with my life which sometimes it seems may not be worth as much as it used to be, but then, of course, you have to allow for inflation. The point is that Rambam employs a lot of extralegal tricks that he can get away with because he works as a lone wolf. A wolf is not a dog. You can't teach a wolf to sit. Kent does not employ clever stratagems; he employs a large staff of people and delegates authority like a military field general. Believe me, he's the man for the job. Kent Perkins will not only resurrect my damaged credibility, he'll pursue this investigation as my proxy agent, and he'll follow this matter to its logical conclusion. I'll bet you a million cans of sliced chicken in gravy."

The cat was not a betting person. Nor did she know or give a shit about knowing Kent Perkins. These days, indeed, she seemed only knowledgeable of two things: how to lick her anus and how to irritate the Kinkster, both of which she was presently engaged in.

"Stop licking your anus!" I yelled.

"Sorry, mate," said a voice. "Didn't realize you were up."

"Hi, Piers," I responded weakly.

"Some may think I'm an asshole," said Piers, "but I reckon I haven't been licking my anus."

"I was talking to the cat."

"The cat doesn't appear to have been licking her anus recently either. Look for yourself. She's sound asleep in the rocking chair."

"So she is," I said.

Had I been talking to the cat all this time or had I merely been talking to myself? I didn't really know the answer. Was I simply a man talking to a cat or was I drifting dangerously back and forth between reality and some semi-state of delirium?

"I'm worried about you, Kinkster," said Piers. "Having been born and raised in New Guinea, I have seen the effect a prolonged case of malaria can have upon a man. Sometimes the victim never quite comes back, if you know what I mean. I've seen, in fact, several examples of this phenomenon occur in the tropics, resulting in the victim of the disease remaining emotionally unbalanced for the remainder of his often short and typically very unpleasant life. If they conquer the malaria, sometimes they remain in the category of the walking wounded, just a pathetic set of barely ambulatory skeletal remains."

I loved the way Piers pronounced the word "skeletal." He

placed the emphasis on the second syllable and made the word rhyme with "beetle."

"We're not in the tropics," I reminded him. "This is New York."

"I know that. And you know that, mate. But the question is does the *Plasmodium falciparum* know it?"

"So what do you want me to do, Piers? Check into a fucking mental hospital?"

"Take a look around at this place and some of its inhabitants and I'd reckon you're already there, mate."

"You've got a point. McGovern did clean up the cat turds this afternoon though."

"Well, he did a shithouse job, mate. Take those opera glasses and check out this floor. If your cat were the size of a Bengal tiger she couldn't have deposited this many droppings or this quantity of manure in one evening. I think McGovern's part of the problem, mate."

"You're right. On the other hand, good help is hard to get."

"The kind of help you might need, mate, I'm not sure McGovern, Brennan, or Ratso can give you. I'm not sure I can provide it either."

"What do you mean?" I said uneasily.

Piers walked over to the refrigerator, opened it, took out two bottles of Victoria Bitter, deftly removed the caps, and handed one bottle to me. He drank about half of his VB in one swig. I sipped mine a bit more conservatively, ever mindful of my condition. Piers put his hand on my shoulder and looked me right in the eyes.

"I've known you a long time, Kinkster," he said. "Suzanne and I thought highly enough of you to make you the godfather of our daughter Pia."

I nodded numbly. I had no idea where Piers was going with this rather out-of-character soliloquy, but it sounded serious. I took a bigger gulp of my VB.

"What I'm telling you, Kink, is that I've seen you at your best and I've seen you at your worst, but I've never seen you like this. I think you may need professional help."

"Interesting that you say that," I said. "Great minds think alike, I guess. I was going to keep this a secret, but, as you may know, the only secrets I've kept are the ones I've forgotten."

"Very true, mate."

"Anyway, you know Kent Perkins from L.A.?"

"Of course. Tall, blond Norouija board."

"Yes, well, he's now got his own detective agency and he's coming to New York next week to help me find out the truth about what happened across the street the other night. I can't leave the loft, and I can't rely on a bunch of doubting Thomases like the Village Irregulars to be of much assistance either. Kent's ready to help me tackle the job and he's a true professional."

"That wasn't what I was referring to when I said you might need professional help, mate."

"You don't think Kent's a professional private investigator?"

"I was talking about another kind of professional help, mate."

"Like?"

"Like a shrink or a psychiatric nurse."

Suddenly the loft became quiet as a tomb. I was about ready to shit standing. Piers Akerman, one of my oldest, most trusted friends, with a level of maturity far exceeding that of most of the American members of the Village Irregulars, now was seriously doubting my sanity. A shrink or a psychiatric nurse. Fuck him and the koala he rode in on!

Possibly sensing my rising anger, Piers did not say a word. Instead, he turned and went to the refrigerator, from which, not surprisingly, he extracted another VB and proceeded to drink the entire bottle while I stood there in a state of shock, still reeling from his suggestion. Piers, who had many Aussie friends who shit in women's purses, took out their penises at every inappropriate moment, and carried on in the most outlandish behavior on the freaking face of the earth, thought I was crazy.

"I'm going to take a shower," said Piers. Still standing by the window in stunned disbelief, I watched him aim his large, antipodean torso toward the rain-room, as if nothing at all had happened.

I didn't know whether to kill myself or get a haircut. If Ratso or McGovern or Brennan had made the same indictment of my mental condition, it very likely might have glossed right over my shoulders, but coming from Piers, it hit me like a bullet to the heart. Piers was one of the few people I knew who, though younger than me, I'd always looked to for wisdom and advice. Piers, who was almost never serious about anything, now was being very serious, indeed. His words had angered me, confused me, saddened me, surprised me, and yes, even frightened me. In an odd way, I thought, it was a tribute to a man that his words could have such a profound effect upon a friend. That was the trouble. Piers was a friend. And I was, very possibly, a crazy man, standing at a lonely window.

I don't know how long I stood there like that. Alone, all alone.

The cat was still sleeping peacefully on the rocker. The sounds of Piers's shower like rain falling on the roof of a boxcar in a dream, on the track to Nowhere, Alabama. Then, like Hank Williams himself, I saw the light.

The building across the street was dark and I could see the light clearly, like a lantern in an old church tower, like a lighthouse at sea, a cross on a hill. I knew in my gut that the light was illuminating the same apartment I'd seen before. I grabbed the opera glasses and focused on the window of the place. I saw the table. I saw the flowers in the vase. Then I saw the guy. The same guy. But I didn't see the woman.

The guy was sitting at the table, doing something I couldn't quite see. His hands were on the table; they were busy, but it didn't look like he was eating. More like he was putting together a puzzle or something. Then he stood up and moved a little closer to the window. He turned slightly and I now could see him fairly clearly in profile. He was holding something in his hands. Suddenly, I knew what it was.

"Jesus Christ!" I shouted to a sleeping cat and a showering Piers Akerman. "He's got a gun!"

I ran for the rain-room like a man possessed. The door was locked and I banged on it with all my might, yelling repeatedly for Piers. At long last, the door opened and out through the steam came Piers Akerman like a stampeding bull elephant with a towel around its waist.

"What the hell is it, mate?" he said. "Is the flat on fire?"

"He's got a gun!" I shouted. "He's standing at the window, the light is on, and he's holding a gun!"

I shoved the opera glasses into Piers's large hand and we both rounded the corner frantically, narrowly navigating the corridor between the kitchen counter and the refrigerator. Piers almost slipped once and I was very nearly hockey-checked by the espresso machine, but at last, we both reached the window. Piers put the glasses to his eyes, but I could already see that it was too late. The entire front facade of the building was in almost total darkness. The warehouse across the street looked as black as the sea at night under a moonless, starless sky. Where moments earlier I'd seen the lighted apartment, the man with the gun, now there was nothing to be seen. Nothing at all. Piers slowly removed the opera glasses from his eyes.

"Hmmmmm," he said.

CHAPTER NINETEEN

The next day, at the crack of noon, Ratso and I seemed to be the only souls stirring about the loft. The cat was still asleep on my bed, having had a rather active night chasing cockroaches and, as Ratso didn't waste a second to tell me, depositing a fresh Nixon on his backpack. McGovern was in a coma on the couch. Piers and Brennan had gone early in the morning to that place where people say they go when they have that thing that they call a job.

"I can't believe that fucking cat took another dump on my backpack," said Ratso, as he kicked the espresso machine into gear.

"Pinch yourself," I said.

"I tell you, that fucking cat is anti-Semitic."

"That's not true, Ratso. Don't personalize the incident. The cat's not anti-Semitic. She's antieverything."

"Maybe the cat's not antieverything. Maybe she's merely projecting *your* attitudes toward the rest of us."

"That's also possible," I said.

"Well, get over it. Dr. Skinnipipi wants you to stay put and, speaking on behalf of all of the Village Irregulars, we intend to make sure that that's what happens."

"Fuck Dr. Skinnipipi and the bedpan he rode in on."

"Now there's a mature attitude. No wonder Brennan calls you the Jewish Patient."

"Fuck Brennan and the tripod he rode in on. Do we have anything for breakfast besides leftover take-out cartons of squid and pickled vegetables from Big Wong's?"

"Of course! I did some shopping yesterday. Borrowed your credit card. Hope you don't mind. I've got some fresh bagels."

"The bagels are decaying."

"The only thing that's decaying is McGovern's mind. Have you noticed his apparent selective hearing? Sometimes he can hear things fine and sometimes he can't hear shit. It's got to be some kind of pathological trigger mechanism, either conscious or unconscious. It's one of the most irritating and sick things I've ever seen."

"Say again? What? Your dick's caught in the espresso machine?"

"Don't start," said Ratso. "He's sleeping on the couch over there. He might hear you."

"He can't hear anything!" I said in a louder voice. "Except when he wants to!"

"Shhhh. Don't wake him up. It's a pleasant, peaceful morning.

I'll toast a few bagels and we'll have some espresso. It'll be just like old times."

It was a nice Ratsolike sentiment, actually. "Just like old times." It was, however, a sentiment that, in all good faith, I could not really share. There was an elephant in the room, you see. And I wasn't merely referring to McGovern. The fact is, I was pretty sure that Piers had already spoken to Ratso and if he hadn't, he would soon. All of them seemed to be reinforcing each other against me. They were probably all in it together. Dr. Skinnipipi, the cops, and my supposed friends. This was not good old-fashioned New York paranoia on my part. It was a concerted campaign to discredit me, disbelieve me, and disrespect me. It was better, of course, than being dismembered, which was no doubt what could be currently happening to the woman across the street.

The dynamic occurring in the loft was nothing new in the world. Once people begin to think of you as a patient you cease to be thought of as a person. But just because I wasn't a person any longer did not mean that I wasn't a human being. I could see the subtle changes in the behavior of my erstwhile friends. The hesitancy. The dismissiveness. The questioning glances shot back and forth to one another when they thought I wasn't looking. Yes, I was obviously delirious at times. I was also seeing the world and reality in a new and different fashion, courtesy of Malaria Airlines. And one of the landscapes I was observing, with the practiced and penetrating eye of the detective, was an endless dusty plain fraught with the fragility and the futility of the human condition.

"So what do you think of Piers's idea, Kinkstah?" said Ratso, as he brought over a tray of bagels and espresso. His words and his gestures seemed stilted, unctuous, and solicitous.

"I think it's great," I said. "What is it?" I wasn't going to make it easy for him.

"You know. He said he brought it up to you last night."

"Oh, yeah. You mean Piers's idea that he should be the one to sleep on the couch because he's known me longer than McGovern? I believe he also stated that he's responsible for introducing me to McGovern, which is certainly something to be proud of for an adult male Australian currently living on this planet. There is, of course, the small matter of getting McGovern off the couch first. This maneuver may require a forklift or possibly a team of Lilliputian engineers."

"Kinkstah, Kinkstah, Kinkstah," said Ratso, while eating a bagel at the same time.

"I hate it when people say your name three times like that. It means they think you're fucking up and they feel sorry for you but they don't know how they can help. Is that about it?"

"Kinkstah, Kinkstah, Kinkstah, Kinkstah, Kinkstah," said Ratso. "What're we going to do?"

"I know what I'm going to do. I'm going to throw up if you keep treating me like a sick child."

"That's what you're behaving like!" shouted Ratso.

"No, I'm not!" I shouted.

"Look," said Ratso, in only a slightly more conciliatory tone. "You're like that little fucking kid in that fucking movie. You see dead people and you talk to them. I know this. I've watched you conversing with them as you're lying in bed almost every night this week."

"You saw 'em, too, did you?"

"No, I didn't. They're not there! That's the whole point! Now you see a guy beat up some woman. Now you see a guy with a gun. What do you expect us to believe?"

"No matter how ugly it gets," I intoned, "there's nothing as beautiful as the truth."

"Well, it's gotten pretty ugly," said Ratso, helping himself to another bagel. "Almost as ugly as the floor of this loft."

"McGovern just cleaned the place up yesterday. I saw him do it. Or don't you believe me?"

"Oh, I believe you. It's just that McGovern's a slob, Brennan's a slob, Piers is a slob, you're a slob, and I'm a slob. What this place needs is a woman's touch."

"Why don't you ask the woman across the street?"

"That's cute, Kinkstah. Maybe it's time I reminded you that the cops couldn't find the man or the woman you supposedly saw. They couldn't even find an apartment on the floor you said it was. So perhaps Piers is right about you getting some—uh—professional help. And I don't mean Kent Perkins. I mean a good shrink you can just talk to. Tell him what you thought you saw. Tell him how everybody's stabbing you in the back. How there's a great conspiracy against you made up of the doctors, the cops, and your old friends. Tell him you're Jesus fucking Christ!"

"Let's not drag Jesus into this. Jesus was a great teacher. He just didn't publish. And it's amazing what a rumor factory this loft is. Yes, Kent Perkins will be arriving soon, just in the nick of time, I might add. And yes, he is a professional, in the narrow sense of the word. But it is I, the amateur, who will be directing his every

111

movement, other than bowel, of course. God loves an amateur! Kent will merely be my eyes! He will merely be my ears! He will merely be my legs!"

"I've seen better legs on a carrier pigeon."

"—as I was saying, Kent will act at my behest, the amateur giving marching orders to the professional—"

"—and marching powder."

"For I have no use for professionals, my dear Ratso, as mere professionals. Kent will be here in the capacity of my friend. I don't require professional help, as you so sensitively put it, of any kind. Remember, my dear Ratso, Ratso, Ratso, it was professionals who built the *Titanic*. It was amateurs who built the Ark."

CHAPTER TWENTY

I had a lot riding on Kent Perkins's much-anticipated arrival in
New York, my success in this rather unusual investigation, my
reputation as a private investigator, my interpersonal relationships, such as they were, and my likelihood of remaining an ambulatory citizen who doesn't have to read a sign every day that says,
"The Next Meal Is Lunch." That is a lot of baggage for one Californian to carry and I just hoped Kent was up to the job. Perkins
was, of course, not a native Californian. He was born and raised in
Texas. As I always like to say, "It's no disgrace to come from
Texas; it's just a disgrace to have to go back there."

With relations what they were in the little loft community, and
my condition what it was, waiting for Kent Perkins soon took on all
the spiritual proportions of *Waiting for Godot*. I was coming to see

his arrival as my last opportunity for resurrection after many days of being crucified by tiny baby ducks. It was becoming clear even to me that I was not getting any better. On the other hand, I was not especially getting any worse. I simply vaselined back and forth between feeling almost normal and then wandering around lost, shivering, delirious, feverish, hopeless, and disoriented in the grip of a ruthless, unforgiving malarial fugue. But the biggest problem was that all my ills, quirks, comments, and foibles were compounded by the fact that I was living my life in a bell jar under the intense, often misguided scrutiny of the Village Irregulars, and there was no escaping them. Once you're in hospital, nuthouse, opium den, marriage, or gay men's choir, it's not so easy to get out again, and even if you're able to, some of the crud invariably rubs off. The loft, I felt, had a little bit of all these institutions going for it, and whatever peace or freedom I'd once felt there now seemed to have dissipated like so many smoke rings crashing themselves to death under the heels of the lesbians. Everybody knew I was not well. Sometimes I even knew it myself. But reality was still reality, and regardless of my fevered, delirious state of mind and body, I fervently felt that I was observing this rare creature more clearly than ever before in my life. Hell, I thought, many people had never even seen it at all.

"Almost time for this poncey bloke from the left coast to be arrivin', innit?" Brennan asked the question casually, but underneath I detected a note of quiet concern.

"He'll get here when he gets here," I said.

"So will Jesus, mate, but there's no point in waitin' up for him, is there? Do you get my meanin'? Should I stick around the flat to meet and greet or should I go out to the pub? That's the question, innit?"

Brennan had been through about a case of Guinness that afternoon and it hadn't seemed to slow him down a bit. If anything, he seemed slightly more dignified than usual. This was saying a lot for Mick because he did not suffer dignity gladly.

"The real question, Mick, is whether you care to get to the bottom of this mess or not?"

"You mean the flat, mate? It's a true no-hoper. You'd have to dig through twelve archaeological layers of cat shite to get to the bottom of it. You'd probably find Troy and Atlantis on the way."

"I always kind of liked Hector and the Trojans. I would've liked to have fought with the Myrmidons. They were ants transformed into soldiers. I'd like to have hosed Helen. I don't know if I'd have enjoyed listening to Achilles always complaining about his heel."

"Bet the Trojans would be proud to know they have a gumboot named after 'em."

"But what about Helen of New York? What's happening to her may be a crime that goes unnoticed by history. And she lives right across the street."

"So you still believe in your fair lady, mate? Maybe the little treacle really exists. I'll give you that, mate. Let's say she does. Not much we can do about it, is there?"

"Maybe there is, Mick."

"Like what, mate?"

"If nothing else, my dear Watson, we can rescue her from Troy."

"Sod the Trojans, mate. I thought we were speaking about Helen of New York, weren't we?"

115

"There's only one Helen, Watson. She represents all womankind and it is the job of mankind to see she is not forever left to twist in the wind on some archaic tenement clothesline, strung out like a medieval banner, hanging there helpless between the sooty alleyways of truth and vermouth."

"Cut the rubbish, Kink. When you start spouting all this Watson shite, it always worries me."

"Et tu, Watson?"

"Sod Watson, I said! You're crook, mate. We're trying to get you well, aren't we? Your bloke better pop in soon or you'll find yourself back in hospital. And this time your room may have rubber walls."

"If it's good enough for van Gogh, it's good enough for the Kinkster."

But Brennan wasn't listening. He'd already placed a fresh can of Guinness in his coat pocket and was headed for the door. The cat and I received his parting words in stoic silence.

"If your cowboy bloke doesn't get here soon," he said from the doorway, "he may as well not come at all. I owe it to you to tell you, Ratso and Akerman have been scheming with that sawbones Skinnipipi. I'd say your days here are numbered, mate. Just a word to the wise, innit?"

After the door closed behind Brennan's low-to-the-ground, wise Irish ass, the cat and I looked at each other. We'd been expecting something like this, so it was no surprise to either of us really.

"Too bad they don't make Gourmet Last Supper cat food," I said.

The cat, of course, said nothing. Cats do not like to be double-crossed by people they thought were their friends and they see no humor in this traitorous behavior whatsoever. Indeed, they see no humor in anything whatsoever. That's why we call them cats. That's why they don't trust anybody. That's why they never laugh at their own jokes.

Darkness was falling on the city and it seemed to be falling on my life as well. I glanced over at the ragged old davenport and I noticed that McGovern had left the building. It was almost uncanny how a large human being like McGovern could slip away like a thief in the night and not be observed by a great detective like myself. Maybe I was missing something. Maybe I was not seeing things clearly. Maybe I was already crazier than the guy who thinks he's Napoleon.

"What if I *am* Napoleon?" I said to the cat.

The cat did not respond. Or maybe she did respond. However you chose to look at it, the question was barely out of my mouth when she launched herself almost violently into a new campaign of licking her anus.

"Stop licking your anus!" I shouted. The cat, of course, said nothing. This did not terribly surprise me. It's not the easiest thing in the world to speak when you're busy licking your anus.

"Why?" I cried. "Why are you doing it? Is it because you don't like rhetorical questions or because you don't like dictators?"

The cat now stretched and began walking rather dismissively away from me and toward the kitchen window. I got out of the chair and followed, continuing to try to reason with her. There was already enough misunderstanding in the loft and the world, I felt.

"Why can't we all just get along?" I asked.

117

It was, of course, another rhetorical question. It wasn't even original. What was the matter with me, I wondered? Why did I continue to constantly hector the cat with rhetorical questions when I knew very well how much she despised them? It wasn't easy being a cat, I reflected. Dead dictators hated you for being independent. Sanctimonious Buddhists refused to include you in religious paintings of the animal kingdom. Delirious, wild-eyed cowboy Jews from Texas followed you around badgering you with rhetorical questions. Dogs barked, cars roared, garbage trucks grumbled. Large mammals came into your home and never left. Hell, whatever happened to playing with a ball of yarn?

I stood at the kitchen window, looking down at another narrow, lonely Vandam Street night, while dawning in my troubled mind was the realization that anyone who spends his time futilely attempting to empathize with an antisocial cat must, indeed, be sicker than he thinks. It was just about at that moment that I saw her. She was running down the middle of the street toward Hudson. She was running like a crazy woman. I didn't need the opera glasses to know, perhaps instinctively, that she was the same one I'd seen before.

I glanced quickly at the building across the street. The light was on again in the apartment. Inside, I could see a dark, ill-defined figure pacing back and forth like a man in a cage, like the Wild Man from Borneo, doomed, determined, desperate to break out into the smoky night.

Chapter Twenty-one

They say an apple a day keeps a doctor away. Sometimes in life, however, it takes a little bit more than that. I was well enough to realize that leaving the loft would be against the doctor's orders and would further exacerbate my condition, not to mention my relationship with officious bastards like Ratso, McGovern, Brennan, and Piers Akerman. Nevertheless, I was sick enough to instinctively recognize when another soul was in trouble like myself. The girl on the street was obviously not running to catch a bus. She was clearly, to my mind, running for her very life.

I rummaged through the closet, found my old brightly colored Indian jacket and my cowboy hat and boots. The cat stared at me rather quizzically as I hurriedly put on these disparate articles. It was an ensemble that the cat evidently did not appreciate, for she gave a slight, dismissive mew of distaste and walked off in the direction of Ratso's backpack, which, for all practical purposes, had become her happy dumping ground. Cats, as a rule, do not like cowboys. They do, however, heavily empathize with Indians. I've often said, in fact, that all cats are Indians and all dogs are cowboys. Whenever I say this, people usually look at me like I've got a nail in my head. People don't often have big spirits, but most cowboys, Indians, dogs, and cats do. Jerry Lewis, small spirit; Dean Martin, big spirit. The smallest spirits of all, of course, belong to the throngs of German tourists who congregate around American Indian reservations, possibly attempting to heal their psychic wound and suck out the soul they don't inherently possess. If they really knew anything about Indians they'd no doubt realize that Indians do not believe much in ownership or possession. Indians, for instance, do not believe you can own land, or a river, or a dog, or a horse. The only things Indians truly believe you can own are casinos.

You might think that all the above is a fairly involved and convoluted thought process for one to be going through while attempting to get dressed quickly in order to attempt the rescue of a damsel in distress. You'd be wrong again. The busier one is, the busier is one's mind. And though one's movements may be frantic, one's mind may sail true as an arrow. And the unaimed arrow never misses. Especially when it's flying through one's brain at one hundred miles an hour and one has malaria. Too many ones, innit? "You" is better than "one," innit? Let's all go back to you. It's all about you anyway, innit? It's never about me. It's always about you. And at least I realized that I was crazy.

120

To stand at a window dressed in an Indian jacket and a cowboy hat was crazy. To see a lighted apartment across the street and believe some form of evil was emanating from the place was crazy. To grab a cigar out of Sherlock Holmes's head was crazy. To leave the cat in charge was crazy. To have care-givers who were all out getting drunk because they couldn't take care of themselves was crazy. To go against your doctor's orders when you're seriously ill was crazy. And at last I realized that I was *not* crazy. I was, I now believed, quite sane, indeed.

"I'm the only sane man on this train!" I shouted to the cat from the doorway.

The cat, of course, said nothing at all. She knew I was crazy.

All of this took only a matter of moments, and in a few moments more, I was out of the loft, down the stairs, and out of the building for what seemed like the first time since Christ was a cowboy. The cold outside air hit me about the same time as I glanced up at the building across the street. The woman had not been gone long at all, yet the lighted window now seemed to be calling to her through my brain. "Come back, you rotten cunt!" it screamed, seeming to pulsate horror into a world already pregnant with the stuff. I caught myself walking almost robotically toward the building with the intent in mind evidently to throttle the bastard on the third floor. Before I got there, my rational mind convinced my malarial sensibilities that this strategy at this time was probably not best foot forward.

"Go after the girl," said a voice in my head.

"Get back here you fucking bitch!" said another voice.

"You're doing fine, sonny boy," said the voice of my father.

"Kiiinnnnk," said the voice of Kent Perkins.

I ran then, like the wind I was married to. I ran right down the middle of the street toward Hudson, the same direction the girl had run. As I ran I felt the fever running through my soul, carrying me along toward delirium or destiny, or maybe these two imposters inhabited the same scruffy corner of the nighttime street. As I ran I saw dogs and cats and Indians and cowboys and angels. But I could not see the girl.

I ran for miles through a fog-shrouded uncrowded nocturnal valley where newspaper pages blew around the sky like giant tropical leaves that had fallen from trees made of steel. I searched and searched for a woman and saw only gutters and trash and neon lights and windows behind which lived possible people. I saw a black man walk a white dog. I saw a cake someone had left out in the rain. I saw a rat running next to me and I asked the rat if he'd seen a woman and he said he never could see a woman and if they didn't have pussies there'd be a bounty on them and he said I looked like I could use a good meal would I like some spare cheese and I said no thanks I had an apple on the train. Then the rat got into a Mercedes and drove away and I was alone again running, falling, looking for eyes in the city of night.

"Taxi!" said a woman with roulette eyes and a necklace of garbage cans. "Taxi!"

But there was no taxi. Only lights and wheels and pain and a woman.

"What do you want?" she said.

Her face had blood. Her eyes had tears. Her voice had sadness.

"Why are you following me?" she said.

"I saw you," I said, feeling pain in my heart and in my head. "I saw you in the window."

She was the same woman. A different night. A different street. A different man. But she was the same woman. Her eyes remembered.

"Let me help you," I said, reaching for her arm.

"Go away," she said. "Everything's fine. I don't need your help."

"If you go back," I said, "he'll only hurt you worse."

She ran away from me then and I ran and I fell and it started to rain and everything was fine.

CHAPTER TWENTY-TWO

A wise old man named Slim, who wore a paper Rainbow Bread cap, drank warm Jax beer in infinite quantities, listened faithfully on the radio to the hapless Houston Astros, and washed dishes at our family's ranch, once told me something I've never forgotten. He said: "You're born alone and you die alone so you might as well get used to it." It didn't mean much to me then, but over the years I've come to believe that old Slim might have been on to something.

I live alone now in the lodge my late parents once lived in, and I'm getting used to it. Being a member of the Orphan Club is not so bad. Sooner or later, fate will pluck us all up by our pretty necks. If you have a family of your own, maybe you won't feel it quite as much. Or maybe you will. I'm married to the wind and my children are my animals and the books I've written, and I love them all. I don't play favorites. But I miss my mom and dad. In the past fifty years, thousands of kids have known them as Uncle Tom and Aunt Min. They bought our ranch in 1952, named it Echo Hill, and made it into a camp for boys and girls. Echo Hill will be open again this summer, but though the kids will ride horses, swim in the river, and explore the hills and canyons, they will not get to meet Uncle Tom and Aunt Min.

My mother died in May 1985, just a few weeks before camp started, and my father died in August 2002, just a few weeks after camp was over. I can still see my mother at her desk, going over her cluttered clipboard filled with all the camp rosters, schedules, and menus. I can see her at the Navajo campfire, at the big hoe-down on the tennis courts, at the friendship circle under the stars. I can see my dad wearing a pith helmet and waving to the kids in the charter buses through the dust of the years. I can see him raising the flag in the morning, slicing the watermelon at picnic suppers, sitting in a lawn chair out in front of the lodge, and talking patiently with a kid having problems with his bunkmates. If you saw him sitting quietly there, you'd think he was talking to one of his old friends. Many of them became just that.

I don't know how many baby fawns ago it was, how many stray dogs and cats ago, or how many homesick kids ago who came to see Echo Hill as their home, but fifty years is a long time in camp years. Yet time, as they say, is the money of love. And Tom and Min put a lot of all those things into Echo Hill. Most of their adult lives were given over to children, daddy-long-legs, arrowheads, songs, and stars. They lived in a little green valley surrounded by gentle hills, where the sky was as blue as the river, the river ran pure, the waterfalls sparkled clear in the summer sun, and the campfire embers seemed to never really die. I was just a kid then, but looking back, that's the way I remember it.

But what I remember most of all are the hummingbirds. It might have been in 1953 when my mother hung out the first hummingbird feeder on the front porch of the lodge. The grown-up, outside world liked Ike that year and loved Lucy, and Hank Williams died, as did Ethel and Julius Rosenberg. I believe now that I might have been vaguely aware of these things occurring even back then, but it was those tiny wondrous rainbows of flying color that really caught my eye. Those first few brave hummingbirds had come thousands of miles, all the way from Mexico and Central America, just to be with us at Echo Hill. Every year the hummers would make this long migration, arriving almost precisely on March 15, the Ides of March. They would leave late in the summer, their departure date usually depending upon how much fun they had at camp.

For those first few years, in the early fifties, the hummingbird population, as well as the number of campers, was fairly sparse, but as the green summers flashed by, more and more kids and hummingbirds came to Echo Hill. The hummingbirds nested every year in the same juniper tree next to the lodge. Decades later, after my mother's death, the tree began to die as well. Yet even when there were only a few green branches left, the hummers continued to make that tree their summer home. Some of the staff thought the tree was an eyesore and more than once offered to cut it down, but Tom wouldn't hear of it. I think he regarded the hummingbirds as little pieces of my mother's soul.

My father and I more or less took over the hummingbird program together in 1985. As time went by, we grew into the job. It was amazing how creatures so tiny could have such a profound influence upon your peace of mind and the way you looked at the world. My father, of course, did many other things besides feeding the hummingbirds. I, unfortunately, did not. That was how I gradually came to be known as the Hummingbird Man of Echo Hill.

Tom and I disagreed, sometimes almost violently, about the feeding methods for these fragile little creatures. He measured exactly four scoops of sugar and two drops of red food coloring into the water for each feeder. I eyeballed the whole process, using much more sugar and blending many weird colors into the mix. Whatever our disagreements over methodology, the hummer population grew. This past summer, it registered more than a hundred birds at "happy hour." Tom confided in me that once long ago he mixed a little gin in with the hummers' formula and they seemed to have a particularly lively happy hour. Min was not happy about it, however, and firmly put a stop to this practice.

Some bright cold mornings I stand in front of the old lodge, squinting into the brittle Hill Country sunlight, hoping, I suppose, for an impossible glimpse of a hummingbird or of my father or mother. They've all migrated far away, and the conventional wisdom is that only the hummingbirds are ever coming back. Yet I still see my mother hanging up that first feeder. The juniper tree blew down in a storm two winters ago, but the hummers have found other places to nest. One of them is in my heart.

And I still see my dad sitting under the dead juniper tree, only the tree doesn't seem dead, and neither does he. It takes a big man to sit there with a little hummingbird book, taking the time to talk to a group of small boys. He's telling them that there are over three hundred species of hummingbirds. They are the smallest of all birds, he says, and also the fastest. They're also, he tells the kids, the only birds who can fly backward. The little boys seem very excited about the notion of flying backward. They'd like to try that themselves, they say. So would I.

Chapter Twenty-three

"To feed a hummingbird," I said softly to the cat. I was back in my bed, I supposed. The cat said nothing, I supposed. Pretty much what I'd expected, I supposed.

It was very similar to being a child again, I thought. Waking up in the middle of the night and maybe you'd done something wrong or maybe you hadn't. You weren't sure. But you could hear the adults talking in the next room. And every word they spoke seemed to be so important, falling like a raindrop through the long dark night of childhood onto the window of your heart.

"So how'd you get him into the soddin' building, mate?"

"I carried him," said the confident voice with the warm, friendly Texas drawl. "I found him down the block lying in the gutter in the rain. I carried him back here and put him in bed. The best thing to do now is let him sleep."

"But how'd you get into the soddin' building, mate? How'd you get into the soddin' flat?"

"Your security system's a bit lax, and I don't mean the airport. But there was really nothing to it. I don't usually make a practice of breaking and entering, but I am a licensed detective and, in fact, I have my own agency in California. That's the long, sort of banana-shaped state on the left coast of America. You've heard of America, haven't you?"

"We settled you, mate. Back several hundred years ago when we were all puritanical pilgrims just tryin' to plow some Indian maidens."

"You didn't do a very good job, mate," said Piers Akerman's booming voice. "Settling or plowing. You mucked up Australia as well."

"And don't be fucking our maidens," said McGovern loudly. "I'm part Indian, too."

"Which part, mate?" said Brennan.

"This part," said McGovern.

The sounds of a large drunken Irishman and a small, scrappy, and equally drunken Brit scuffling in a loft beneath the pounding feet of a recently activated lesbian dance class could clearly be heard. After a few moments, however, cooler heads apparently prevailed. I could hear Kent Perkins's calming voice bringing everything under control.

"Fellas," he said. "Fellas. This isn't getting us anywhere. We all want the same thing, don't we? To help the Kinkster get well and help him resolve his latest investigation and determine if, indeed, a crime has occurred. To do that we'll have to all work together."

Kent, I knew, had several rules of investigation and interrogation and one of them he'd borrowed from my father. That was to always treat children like adults and adults like children, and it seemed to be working very well on this particular occasion. Listening to Kent from the bedroom, you might have thought he was speaking to a kindergarten class.

"McGovern will fuck things up, mate," piped up Mick Brennan.

"No, I won't, you poison dwarf!" responded McGovern. "*You* will!"

"Bollocks!"

"Now, now," said Perkins soothingly. "This won't get us anywhere. Let me tell you what Kinky was mumbling to me about as I carried him in from the rain."

"I wouldn't put too much stock in it," said Ratso. "The Kinkstah's been mumbling weird shit ever since the day he got out of the hospital."

"Joan of Arc heard voices in her head," said Kent. "As a result, she was able to save the entire nation of France."

"Pity," said Ratso.

"All right now," said Kent. "Let's focus in on the investigation. Since I met Piers years ago with Kinky in L.A., I'm going to make him second in command."

"That's a mistake," said McGovern. "He's blind as a kangaroo."

"He's one of those anti-Aussie bigots," said Piers. "He can't hear a word that's been said."

"What?" said McGovern. "What about tickets to the Grateful Dead?"

"See what I mean?" said Piers. "He's a true no-hoper."

"All right now," said Kent. "Piers will be second in command and Kinky's told me wonderful things about you other Village Irregulars."

"Bollocks!" said Brennan. "You haven't even talked to Kinky about us."

"Yes I have," said Kent. "Kinky said you guys can can piss off a Good Humor Man. He says you're the original gang who can't shoot straight. He also says you're the best, most loyal friends he's got in the world and he wouldn't hesitate to trust you with his life."

There was a long silence in the loft. Even the lesbian dance class seemed to stop in its tracks. The cat looked at me rather quizzically. I shrugged.

"We're doing this investigation for three reasons," said Kent. "One is for Kinky. At a time when he's so weak and delirious, he needs to have evidence that something of a criminal nature really is occurring across the street. In other words, his mental health and his own self-worth require some kind of proof that he's not insane."

"What if he is, mate?" asked Brennan, not unreasonably.

"Well," said Kent, "does anyone here have any background in psychology?"

"I do," said Ratso. "I've got a master's in psychology from the University of Wisconsin at Madison."

"Why didn't you go ahead and get your Ph.D.?" asked Kent.

"A spider bit me on the scrotum," said Ratso.

"I see," said Kent. "Well, you still have the most training of anyone here. We'll certify you as house shrink. Do you think at this moment that Kinky's insane?"

There was silence for a longer time than I would have wished as Ratso evidently grappled with the question. At last, he came up with an answer that was not a strong vote of confidence for the general state of my mental hygiene.

"No, I don't think he's really insane," said Ratso, rather uncertainly. "At least not yet."

"Okay," said Kent. "You watch him closely, Ratso. If you think we need to call in a shrink, we will. In the meantime, let's give him the benefit of the doubt. Now the second reason for the investigation is that if there really is an abused woman across the street, her life may be in mortal danger. Sometimes you just have to have a knack for knowing if something's worth doing, if someone's worth loving, if an investigation's worth taking on. I've brought a spotter scope and some other equipment out here with me, so obviously I believe this one is. Sometimes you can see things clearly in life and sometimes you just have to go with your gut instinct.

"There was a guy I knew over thirty years ago named Joe back in Azle, Texas, outside of Fort Worth. He could lie on his back on the floor of a bar and spit chewin' tobacco high enough to hit the ceiling. Joe was in the septic tank business and on his truck he had a sign that read: 'Your Shit Is My Bread and Butter.'"

"Where's this going, mate?" asked Piers.

"Yeah," said McGovern, "what's a slit who's a ball-cutter got to do with this?"

"'Your Shit Is My Bread and Butter,'" repeated Kent.

"Your clit runs a bed and breakfast?" asked McGovern, who was not only not hearing very well, but was also, apparently, drinking rather heavily.

"Now another friend of mine back then," continued Kent

135

smoothly, "was a guy named Gary Lynn who started a printing business and on his truck he had a sign that said: 'We Print Everything But Money.' Well, the printing business was going a little slow so Gary thought he'd try his hand at printing twenty-dollar bills. And he got pretty good at it so one day he thought he'd see if he could pass them off for the real thing. He got in his truck and drove over a hundred miles up into Oklahoma and found this little gas station in this little town up there. He bought gas from the old man at the little station and bought some other stuff and paid for it all with one of the twenties. Then he got back in his truck and drove back to Azle where the cops were waiting to arrest him. What he didn't know was that the old man had only recently bought that gas station because he'd gotten bored after retiring from his other job. His other job, to which he'd devoted most of his adult life, was as a counterfeit investigator for the U.S. Treasury Department."

"What's the moral of the story, mate?" said Brennan.

"I told you this was a hard room to work," said Piers.

"The moral is," said Kent with a bit of irritation, "some things are written on trucks so they can even be seen by shmucks."

"Hey!" shouted McGovern. "You said there were three reasons for the investigation. What's the third?"

"The third reason for the investigation is that you guys have made me so mad I'll do it all by myself if I have to."

I could hear the murmur of the Village Irregulars as they consulted, chided, sucked, fucked, and cajoled each other. Finally, they spoke in turn.

"I'll help you," said Ratso.

"I'm with you, mate," said Brennan.

"I'm always with you, mate," said Piers.

"What fucking little leprechaun took the Jameson?" said McGovern.

"All right," said Kent. "We'll spread out some sleeping bags and get some sleep tonight. But we hit the ground running tomorrow. You never know what's going to happen when you get into an investigation. So what we do, we do with all our hearts."

A small cheer went up from the living room. It was rather poignant but very heartening for me to hear and it lifted my spirits considerably. Only the cat looked at me with doubt in her eyes.

"So give it all you've got," said Kent. "Remember what my daddy back in Texas used to say?"

"What was that, mate?" said Brennan.

"Never save your best shirt for Sunday," said Kent.

CHAPTER TWENTY-FOUR

The next morning Ratso brought me coffee, juice, and a few of my medications. He carried them into the bedroom on a tray, like a child might serve breakfast in bed to his mother on mother's day. There was something so sad, so poignant about this act that it almost made me cry. Ratso never knew his birth mother, and his adoptive mother, Lilyan, was currently in a Florida nursing home. My mother had flown off with the hummingbirds in 1985. If the cat found anything touching about this little scenario of Ratso bringing in the coffee on a tray, she wasn't showing any of her cards. She merely sat on the pillow next to me, glaring at Ratso as if he were a dog from hell.

"Great news!" said Ratso. "Guess who's setting up in the kitchen?"

"Martha Stewart?"

"Pete Myers! Myers of Keswick, Kinkstah! Brought about a month's supply of British gourmet shit! Scones! Those little rolls with sausage in them! A whole side of beef! That hot British mustard you like!"

"I'm not hungry, Ratso."

"Well, you should be, after that great escape you pulled last night. You weren't really thinking—running out in the rain like that, were you, Kinkstah?"

"I saw the girl. I saw the girl running. And her face was all bloody."

"Of course you did. Then apparently you must have passed out in the gutter. That's where Kent Perkins found you."

"I'm well aware of that."

"Hold the weddin', Kinkstah. Kent said you were unconscious from the time he found you until the time he put you to bed. How'd you know about that?"

"I happened to overhear your little war council last night."

"No one likes an eavesdropper, Kinkstah."

"I'm not a fucking eavesdropper! It's my fucking loft!"

"And you're going to stay the fuck in it from now on until you're well!"

"We'll see," I said, winking broadly to the cat.

The cat, of course, said nothing. But her baleful glare could have withered Ratso's entire flea market wardrobe. Cats sometimes seem to forget their friends. But they never forget their enemies. And they might just be on to something there.

"Just take it easy, Kinkstah," said Ratso, in his best psychological, conciliatory tone. "Have some coffee. It's not good to get too excited in your condition."

"Fine," I said. "What's all the racket in the living room?"

"Kent and Mick are setting up the spottah scope, Pete's grinding sausage, Piers is taking a shower, and McGovern's snoring on the couch."

"Kent and Mick are setting up what?"

"Some dingus Kent brought with him. The spottah scope."

"Oh. The *spotter* scope."

"That's what I said, Kinkstah. The spottah scope."

"And here's what I have to say, Ratso. At last, we'll see."

It was later that morning when Kent Perkins came into my invalid's quarters and told me that he thought it might be necessary to attempt to hypnotize me. I didn't really have any strong religious opposition to the idea and, at this point, anything that might further the investigation was fine with me. Any personal risk or sacrifice would be fine, I told him. Anything for the team.

Kent told me that he appreciated my attitude and that it was just barely possible that this particular rag-tag group of jaded, degenerate individuals might actually turn into a team. Either that, he said, or things were going to turn pretty ugly. Pretty ugly, indeed.

"You know, Kent," I said, as I shivered under several layers of comforters, "all of us working together on this investigation reminds me of a story our friend Ted Mann told me once. It's about the famous ancient Greek sculptor Polyclitus."

"Polyclitus? Never heard of him."

"Neither had I. Only Ted Mann has heard of him. Anyway, he decided once that he'd create two statues at the same time, one of which he'd let the public watch and—interactively you might say—participate in its construction. The other, however, was a private affair, and he kept it wrapped in tarpaulins, and only worked on it late at night when he was alone."

"This sounds like a Ted Mann story."

"Anyway, as Polyclitus was working on the first statue, people would look at it and say: 'You know, that thigh seems a little too short.' And Polyclitus would dutifully lengthen the thigh of the statue. And people would say: 'You know, you don't have the eyes quite right.' And Polyclitus would go to work on the statue's eyes. And so on. Then, late at night, he'd work on the second statue all by himself. At any rate, he finished work on both pieces at about the same time and he took them out to the public square in Athens and mounted them, not sexually, of course, in the square for everybody to see.

"When the public saw the first statue, the one he'd permitted them to have a hand in creating, they openly mocked and ridiculed it as an inferior piece of sculpture. But, ah, the second statue, the one he'd done on his own, this they hailed as a masterpiece, as a great transcendental work of art. And they asked Polyclitus, 'How could it be that one statue was so good and the other was so bad?' And Polyclitus answered: 'Because *I* did this one, and *you* did that one.'"

"And that's why," said Kent, "you'll never see a statue erected to a committee."

"That's also why," I said, "you'll never see a penis erected to a committee."

"Kiiinnnnnk."

CHAPTER TWENTY-FIVE

And thus it was, swaddled like the Baby Jesus, with my two disciples, Ratso and McGovern, supporting me in my weakened state, that I was ushered into the living room of the loft later that afternoon and placed rather delicately in a warm chair beside the roaring fire in the fireplace. I hadn't been in the front room in a while and now I found the place to be humming with activity and kind of homey as well. Pete Myers was busily slicing thin, delicious-looking pieces of rare roast beef. Brennan was assiduously adjusting the tripod of the spotter scope, which now stood like a sentinel at the kitchen window. Kent Perkins was typing some information into his laptop at my desk. Almost as soon as I was placed in the chair, the cat jumped up in my lap and curled up and made herself comfortable there. I hated to say it, but I almost felt like I was at home.

"Well," said Piers, walking over with a large can of Foster's in his large hand, "what's our next amusement?"

"Our next amusement," said Kent, "is I'm going to attempt to hypnotize Kinky and draw out a little more information about the battered woman he chased down on the street last night."

"That's rich," laughed Brennan. "Some bloke pounds the shite out of her and then she tries to run away and she sees this wild-eyed bloke in a black cowboy hat and red Indian blanket chasin' after her in the rain."

"This wild-eyed bloke sitting peacefully by the fire here," said Kent, "might just unknowingly hold the key to saving that poor woman's life."

"Garrison Keillor's made of cat shit," I said.

"Holds the key to saving her life?" said Brennan. "Not likely, mate."

"Give the man a chance, lad," said Pete Myers, as he arranged the counter into a sumptuous buffet worthy of an English manor house. "The human mind holds secrets within secrets."

"The only secrets the Kinkstah's ever kept," said Ratso, "are the ones he's forgotten."

"Those are precisely the ones we're going to try to find," said Kent, as he got out from behind the desk and advanced confidently toward the fireplace. "Are you ready, Kink, to do a little bit of time traveling?"

"Orson Welles is made of cat shit," I said.

"He means H. G. Wells," said Piers. "He wrote *The Time Machine.* George Orwell wrote *Animal Farm,* which this loft is rapidly coming to resemble."

"At least he got the 'Wells' part right," said Kent. "Let's see what else he remembers."

With that, Kent reached over to the fireplace mantel and smoothly removed the little wooden puppethead. He swung it back and forth a few times like a pendulum, holding the parachute between his thumb and index finger.

"This little black head ought to work," said Kent. "What's it here for? Is Kinky trying to start a collection of American Negro memorabilia?"

"That little puppethead," said Piers pontifically, "is the way most of us ordinary citizens use to enter the building. Those of us, that is, who are not private investigators from Los Angeles. The puppethead is thrown from yon kitchen window, falls in a slight trajectory—"

"Every rock has a trajectory," I said, quoting my father's message to the kids at camp each summer. "Don't throw rocks."

"—falls in a slight trajectory," continued Piers, "into the waiting hands of the potential visitor or housepest. You will observe, of course, as a detective, that the key to the building is wedged firmly in the little smiling mouth of the Negro puppethead. The visitor then extracts said key from said mouth, utilizes it to open the doors of the building, legs it up four floors, and, if admitted to this loft, hands it to the particular care-giver in charge, who then replaces it where you found it, upon the mantel of the fireplace."

"Novel idea," said Kent.

"Piers Akerman's made of cat shit," I said.

"That's why I made him my number-two man," said Kent. "Okay, Kink, let's get started. Now I learned the technique I will be employing from one of the greatest hypnotists in the world, John Kappas, who also happened to be married to a friend of mine and Ruthie's, Florence Henderson."

"What?" said McGovern. "Say again? He was married to Skitch Henderson?"

"No, McGovern," said Ratso. "Florence Nightingale was married to Hollywood Henderson."

"Is John Kappas alive or dead?" asked Piers.

"He's dead," said Kent.

"He was swinging a gold watch back and forth," said Brennan, "and he hit himself in the forehead."

"Can we get on with this now?" said Kent. "I finally understand what it's like to be Florence Henderson. You guys are worse than the *Brady Bunch*."

"You and Florence Henderson have something else in common," said Brennan, who'd been drinking. "You're both bloody cunts."

"The Von Trapp Family Singers are made of cat shit," I said.

"Block out everything," said Kent. "Watch this puppethead. I'm going to count down from ten to one and you're going to get very, very sleepy."

I watched Kent Perkins slowly swinging the little puppethead back and forth in an arc in front of my face. I watched the puppethead. The cat watched the puppethead. We both started to become very, very sleepy. It's a funny thing about hypnosis, but whether you believe in it or not, a puppethead in the right hands always seems to do the trick.

"Ten," said Kent Perkins. "Nine . . . eight . . . seven . . . six . . . your eyelids are getting heavy, very, very heavy."

I no longer knew about the cat, but my own eyelids were getting very, very heavy. The puppethead kept swinging back and forth like some kind of cosmic cradle, rocking to and fro with the inexorable certainty of the tides and the seasons, back and forth like love and hate and death and life itself and I saw Robert Louis Stevenson drowning on a shipwrecked vessel flying the Jolly Roger and I saw Edgar Allan Poe dying in a gutter or maybe I didn't see anything at all.

"Five," said Kent, "four, three, two, one. I could make him jack off like a monkey right now. Okay, Kink. Now you're back in the loft standing right over there by the kitchen window. It's dark on the street. It's late at night. You're all alone here in the loft and you look down at the street. Now tell me what you see."

"Garbage trucks," I said. "Just garbage trucks."

"Are the garbage trucks picking up garbage?"

"No. They're sleeping."

"Okay. Do you see anything else?"

"I see a homeless man."

"You see a homeless man. What is the homeless man doing?"

"The homeless man is urinating on a lamppost. The urine looks beautiful and translucent in the lamplight."

"Okay. Do you see anything else on the street?"

"I see a dog. A stray dog. He looks lost and lonely and sad and brave and beautiful. The cat also sees the dog. The cat doesn't like the dog. But I like the dog. I think the dog may contain a piece of the spirit of Jesus Christ."

"Okay. Do you see anything else?"

"I see an empty street and an empty sidewalk and an empty life."

"You see an empty life? Is it your life?"

"Maybe it's mine. Maybe it's everybody else's. I don't know yet."

"When you find out, be sure and tell me."

"I will."

"Okay. It's dark and you and the cat are still standing by the window looking down into the street. Is it still empty?"

"Yes. It's still—no! There's a woman running down the middle of the street. It's starting to rain but she's not running from the rain. She's running *to* the rain."

"Have you ever seen this woman before?"

"Yes."

"Where have you seen her?"

"In the lighted window across the street."

"When did you first see her?"

"A long time ago. Two weeks ago."

"What was she doing?"

"She was standing in the light. He came in and beat her. I called the cops. They came and investigated and said there was no apartment on that floor and nobody'd seen or heard anything."

"But you did?"

"I saw him beat her."

"And you saw him another time?"

"Yes. He was standing in the light with a gun."

"And what did you do?"

"I called Piers out of the rain-room but by the time he got to the window everything was dark in the building across the street. He didn't believe me."

"Piers didn't believe you? The others didn't believe you? The cops didn't believe you? Nobody believed you really believed you actually saw anything? That about right?"

"That's right. Nobody believed me."

"I believed you, Kink. I believed you saw what you said you saw."

"I—I hoped you would."

"Now you're back at the window last night and you see the woman running like crazy through the rain. What do you do?"

"I go out after her."

"Why?"

"I want to help her. She's wearing a nice blue dress and it's raining."

"You go out in the street in the rain against your doctor's orders?"

"Fuck Dr. Skinnipipi and the nurse he rode in on."

"That's the spirit! Now, you see the woman running. Can you see the man as well?"

"Yes. He's hurt her again and he's pacing back and forth in his window."

"Yet you leave him there and you go after the woman? Why?"

"I want to save her."

"So you go out into the cold and rainy night and you pursue this strange, frightened creature, and finally you catch up to her. What happened then?"

"She said, 'Taxi!.' She said, 'What do you want?' She said, 'Why are you following me?'"

"And what did you say to her?"

"I said, 'I saw you. I saw you in the window.' I said, 'Let me help you.'"

"What did she say?"

"She said, 'Go away! Everything's fine. I don't need your help.'"

"That's what every abused woman in the world who needs help says at first. Did you do anything then?"

"Yes. I—I grabbed her purse when she wouldn't tell me her name. I wanted to find her name. When I saw her crying there in the rain she reminded me so much of another girl. A girl I used to know. She was surrounded by everything Warren Zevon hated: guns, money, and lawyers, and she was surrounded by everything Warren Zevon loved: drugs, dreams, and lost angels, and she left messages sometimes on my answering machine that she loved me and she was crying and I couldn't reach her across the California night. She was the love of my life and she died alone and I couldn't save her."

"Kacey," said Kent Perkins.

"Kacey," said Piers Akerman knowingly, his voice booming through the cosmos like a somber echo of Kent's.

I was crying now. I could feel the tears on my face. This did not bother me. In fact, it seemed to comfort me. I did not try to wipe away the stream of tears. They felt so natural and right. Like the rain on your face. Like wearing a sad necklace from yesterday.

"So you were trying to save *this* woman?" said Kent. "Well, maybe you have. Did you find her driver's license?"

"Yes."

"What name did you see on that driver's license?"

"Tana Petrich."

"Spell that, please."

"T-a-n-a P-e-t-r-i-c-h."

"Okay. That ought to do it. Now I'm going to count to three and then snap my fingers. When I snap my fingers you're not going to remember any of this. You're going to be relaxed, refreshed, and you're going to feel great. A rather unusual Kinky condition, I might add. Okay. Here we go. One. Two. Three!"

Then Kent Perkins snapped his fingers. Almost before I knew it, I was feeling relaxed, refreshed, and, well, great. Kent pulled another chair up to the desk and Pete Myers brought me a hot and delicious shepherd's pie. As I ate, Kent kicked his computer into overdrive.

"I'm running the name Tana Petrich through peoplefinder.net," he said, laboring like a giant ant over the little laptop. "Peoplefinder.net's a nationwide service available to PIs. It merges data bases so that even if you've only ordered a pizza, you may have left a trail for us to follow."

"Makes you proud to be an American," said Brennan.

"How would you know, lad?" said Pete Myers.

"One thing it does do," said Kent. "It helps you find Tana Petrich in about forty-five seconds."

Kent wasn't off by much. I'd barely gotten my second forkful of shepherd's pie between my choppers when I heard him shouting with excitement.

"We've found the girl!" he ejaculated. "Here she is!"

Ratso, Piers, Brennan, and Pete Myers suddenly gravitated to the desk and began eagerly gazing over Kent's and my shoulders at the little screen. Only McGovern remained snoring away on the couch. Maybe he had the right idea after all.

"One little problem," said Kent. "There's a death claim issued against her name in 1991. A death certificate. This person's been dead for ten years."

"Hmmmmm," said Piers. "What's our next amusement?"

Chapter Twenty-six

The fact that the person you're trying to help appears to be dead can often take the wind out of an investigation. Sometimes, however, it can have the opposite effect. As for myself, I didn't know whether to shit or go blind, but Kent seemed positively galvanized by the sudden turn of events. He appeared to have become obsessed with the inexplicable fact that the woman I'd spoken to on the previous night had apparently been legally dead for over ten years.

"Now we've got ourselves a real investigation," said Kent, as he paced back and forth, repeatedly slamming his fist into his palm with nervous energy. "Now we've got something to sink our teeth into."

"We do?" said Ratso, sinking his teeth into what was left of my shepherd's pie.

"Of course," said Kent ebulliently. "Can't you see it?"

"Can't I see what?" said Ratso.

"Ah, my dear Watson," I said, "your charming naïveté never fails to lend an interesting, if sometimes mildly irritating, feature to an investigation."

"Come on, Sherlock," said Ratso, having finished the shepherd's pie and seamlessly moved on to a hot, open-faced roast beef sandwich, "it's obvious that the woman's a scammer of some kind. She's walking around with a fraudulent driver's license. My opinion, if you want to hear it—"

"But of course, my dear Watson."

"My opinion is that this woman isn't really an abused woman at all."

"And, pray, what might she be, my dear Watson?"

"She could be a terrorist, Sherlock. Do you recall the case several years back that McGovern wrote up in the *Daily News* and dubbed *The Mile High Club?*"

"Of course, Watson, of course. My powers may be failing but how could even a delirious mind forget an adventure like that?"

"You remember the fake passports you cleverly hid in the cat litter, Sherlock?"

"Who could forget an adventure like that?"

"Well, Sherlock, here's a mysterious woman with a fake driver's license. Fake passports. Fake driver's license. The pattern seems quite clear to me. Something about this woman isn't very kosher."

"Something about what you're eating isn't very kosher either, Watson."

"Ah, but I'm not really a practicing Jew, Sherlock."

"True, Watson, true. Or, quite possibly, you just need a little more practice. At any rate, your aforementioned charming naïveté is beginning to become rather predictable and tiresome. You are decidedly a fixed point in a changing age. Unfortunately, my dear Watson, that fixed point is directly on top of your head."

"How's this for an idea? Why don't you go fuck yourself, Sherlock?"

"Ah, how like you, Watson, to respond emotionally to what, of necessity, must remain a rational approach to our little undertaking. The emotional, warm, human component you invariably bring to a case can only serve to obfuscate matters which could more readily be resolved by the deductive reasoning of a cold, scientific mind. Watson, Watson, Watson. I salute your humanity, however misguided that tragic trait may be."

"Fuck you, Sherlock! Fuck you and the cocaine syringe you rode in on!"

Kent Perkins, who'd listened to the entire previous mental hospital conversation in a mute state of mild disbelief, now stood up and placed both hands on top of his head in an attitude of mock surrender.

"Where do I go to give up?" he said. "I can't believe I'm hearing two Jewboys in New York pretending they're Sherlock Holmes and Doctor Watson, two fictional characters who at the very least were latent homosexuals."

"What do you mean 'latent,' mate?" said Brennan. "We've been listenin' to this poofter rubbish a lot longer than you and, believe me, it doesn't get better. Way I see it, mate, is Ratso and the Kinkster are right poncey blokes and this whole investigation's a soddin' load of cobblers."

"Now, just a minute, Mick," said Kent. "I agree with you that Kink and Ratso might do well to drop all this Sherlock-Watson business and give some serious thought to joining the Manhattan Gay Men's Choir. What I don't agree with you about is the investigation."

"Sod the investigation," said Brennan.

"All my little helpers," I said, again quoting my father.

"I'm happy to help investigate, mate," said Brennan. "I just don't understand exactly what it is we're tryin' to investigate."

"I'm a licensed private investigator," said Kent, only half-humorously. "Maybe I can help you."

"No one's ever been able to help Brennan, mate," said Piers. "Many men have died trying."

"And women," put in Pete Myers.

"Sod off, you flamers," said Brennan. "I just asked a simple question of the bloke. What is it that all this combined manpower and brain power is supposed to be investigatin'?"

"Patterns," said Kent. "Ratso was right. There is already a pattern here."

"They don't call me Watson for nothing," said Ratso pridefully.

"Unfortunately," said Kent, "Ratso has misinterpreted the pattern. He's put forth the theory that the woman's false identity on her driver's license indicates that she's some kind of con artist or possibly a terrorist, as was the case with the fake identities Kink once discovered on the passports of real terrorists. The pattern I see, however, is quite different. I see the woman as having a form of repetitive behavior quite common among abused women. I think she changed her identity years ago in order to escape from a previous abusive relationship. Now, still operating under her false identity, she finds herself, as so often happens in these cases, right in the middle of another abusive relationship."

"As I've told you on innumerable occasions, Watson," I said, "we are all creatures of narrow habit."

"Speaking of habit," said McGovern, who'd finally arisen from the couch and now was firing up a large joint and offering it to Kent. "Try some of this."

"What is it?" said Kent.

"Wheelchair weed," said McGovern.

"I'll pass," said Kent. "I've got to keep a clear head."

"I'll try a little of that, mate," said Piers. "I'm second in command."

Piers took the joint, inhaled deeply several times, then handed the joint to Brennan. Brennan inhaled so deeply he just about sucked all the oxygen out of the room. Then he passed the huge doobie to Ratso, who took a dutiful little pull and handed it over to Pete Myers. I don't know what Myers did with it because Kent was now gripping me by the shoulders and forcing me to look directly into his righteously ticked-off countenance.

"*These* are the guys I'm supposed to work with?" he shouted, rather rhetorically, I thought. "*This* is the team I'm supposed to assemble?"

I glanced over at the Village Irregulars. McGovern was firing up another joint. Brennan and Piers were slugging down the Guinness again. Ratso, hardly partaking of either of these vices, was nonetheless following a pattern true to the way of his people. He was eating.

"All my little helpers," I said.

157

Suddenly Kent was standing in the middle of the loft, practically shaking with a fervor that seemed to me very similar to that of a charismatic evangelist preacher. The lesbian dance class in the loft above, which had been particularly brutal all afternoon, now seemed to be thundering on the roof in almost a tribal groove, a heathen counterpoint to Kent's religiosity. Kent raised both arms dramatically and looked toward the heavens. Amazingly, the lesbian dance class fell silent.

"Jesus, Joseph, and Mary!" said McGovern, in a state of stoned awe. "Did you see that?"

"I did, mate," said Piers. "And I'll see your Jesus and raise you a Peter."

Kent, not one to let a momentary advantage slip away, clapped his hands twice, then advanced upon the Village Irregulars like an avenging angel. He stopped only a few paces away from Brennan, who threw his shoulders back and thrust his chin toward Kent in what seemed a rather half-hearted gesture of defiance.

"Don't bow-up on me, son," said Kent, with all the moral authority of a Texas high school football coach. Brennan, in spite of himself, backed down without a word. And like a Texas high school football coach, Kent proceeded to hand out the assignments.

"Okay, Mick," he said, "I want you, with the help of the spotter scope or any other means of your invention, to come up with some solid photographic evidence that this woman and this man across the street actually exist."

"But the Kinkstah's seen both of them," Ratso pointed out.

"But some people don't believe him," said Kent. "The cops don't. Even some of his closest friends don't."

"I believe in fairies," said McGovern, who by this time was very heavily monstered on the wheelchair weed.

"That's because you are one, mate," said Brennan.

"Fuck you, you poison dwarf!"

"Sod yourself, Big Chief Funk-nuts!"

"Ratso's job," continued Kent, seemingly oblivious to the bickering, "will be to nurture, care for, and keep a close eye on Kink here, who, I remind you all, is still a very sick cowboy."

"He's always been a very sick cowboy," said Piers.

"And McGovern's always been a very sick Indian," said Brennan.

"How would you like me to shove that tripod up your ass?" asked McGovern.

"Pete's job is the food—which, by the way, is excellent considering it's British—and the general upkeep of the physical plant, that being the loft."

"I'll not be cleaning up the cat turds, lad," said Pete.

"I'll clean up the fucking cat turds," I said. "It's my cat and my loft and besides, it's very Gandhilike work."

"He's always been a very sick cowboy," said Piers.

"I will, of course, consult regularly with Kink on how the investigation is to be pursued. I think that about wraps it up, gentlemen."

"Wait a minute," said McGovern. "What about me and Piers? What are we? A stoned Indian and a drunken Aussie?"

"Now that you mention it," said Kent. "Just kidding, guys. You two have the most important job of all."

"Great," said Ratso.

"I'm serious," said Kent. "You're both big strong specimens and I suspect you can both be quite charming to the opposite sex when you want to be."

"That's true," said Piers. "At least in my case. What is it exactly that you want McGovern and me to do?"

"Find the girl," said Kent, "and bring her to me."

CHAPTER TWENTY-SEVEN

I did not have a great deal of faith in McGovern's or Piers's abilities to locate the woman who called herself Tana Petrich. I had even less faith in their combined abilities to entice her into that spider web known as 199B Vandam Street. If the truth be told, it's a fairly daunting task to convince any abused woman on the run to come in from the cold. For one thing, they tend not to trust men in general. If they'd started out with this attitude instead of ending up with it, of course, they very likely wouldn't have been abused women in the first place.

While I had my doubts about the Village Irregulars' skills at procuring the woman I'll call Tana, I had no such qualms about Kent Perkins's ability to interrogate her. When it came to good cop–bad cop, he was the best good cop in the world. And he wasn't even a cop. He simply had intuition staked out. He knew people and how to talk to them and how to get the most out of them and how to make them feel relieved and grateful that he'd done so. And he did it all with a comforting Texas drawl, never resorting to violence or strong-arm tactics, never, in fact, even raising his voice.

Kent's interrogative methods were not particularly new or especially original. They were a hodgepodge of Sherlock Holmes, Lieutenant Columbo, dime-store psychology, and cowboy zen savvy. More important, they almost always worked. I'd seen Kent interview people in L.A., often after the cops had already unsuccessfully run them through the wringer. On many occasions, his interviews were responsible for breaking the case. I'd seen veteran homicide detectives simply shake their heads in admiration of his skills for penetrating the mortal facade and finding the human truth.

From actual previous experience, as well as conversations with Kent at many delicatessens in L.A., I pretty well knew where he was coming from, other than, of course, Azle, Texas. I will endeavor here to give you an encapsulation of his philosophy and methodology, which could well be titled: "Rules of the Road for Interrogating Modern Boys and Girls." It might give you some idea why, although admittedly he was like a large, friendly fish out of water in New York, I yet maintained such a high degree of confidence in the abilities of Kent Perkins.

The first rule of Kent's I suspect he borrowed from Nelson Mandela. That is, the guy who gets mad first loses. It took a great deal to get Kent mad in what we like to call normal life; in interrogation mode, it was virtually impossible. His second rule is to pretend he knows your secret already. He just wants to help you. He doesn't need information from you. That's how he always gets information from you. Kent's third rule of interrogation he likes to call "selling the door." In other words, as Kent says, "If you want 'em to stay, tell 'em to leave." It may sound like fairly standard reverse psychology, but before you attempt it, you need to have a finely tuned, intuitive understanding of human nature, or the subject, sure as hell, will bug out for the dugout.

Kent believes you should use a person's attitude to maneuver him to confess. This is very similar, he claims, to the way a judo expert uses the momentum of the other person's punch to throw him to the ground. He also believes in a careful reading of body language. People often scream in body language, he says. You can't ask a question before the person's ready to answer, Kent claims. It's very tough for someone to maintain eye contact when lying. He contends that once the subject tells a lie, he digs in deep and becomes a far more difficult puzzle to decipher. You must stop them before they lie, Kent contends, even if you have to shut them down in midsentence.

There are secrets, of course, that Kent has not told me. These are things that it might be better for you and me, gentile reader, not to know. Being a private investigator is a dirty job and guys like Kent Perkins and Steve Rambam get to do it. One of the most unnerving, depressing, soul-destroying, downright ugly experiences you can have in life is to maintain eye contact, even for a short period of time, with that horrible tar baby we call the human condition.

163

"You know my methods," Kent told me later that evening. "All I require is an opportunity to interview the girl, Tana, and, if possible, I'd like to meet with her abusive boyfriend or husband as well."

"With McGovern and Piers as your chosen procurement agents," I said, "that'll probably occur in the year 2047."

"You have that much confidence in them?" said Kent facetiously. "Or are you going by the Jewish calendar?"

"The Jewish calendar has too many holidays. They'd probably never collar these people for you."

"Well, I'll do some research of my own to find out a little more about Tana Petrich. If I can just get her relaxed and comfortable, I may be able to open her up like a can of smoked oysters."

"And the guy?"

"The guy could be a more thorny problem. We've got to get him to admit that he's been abusive and to understand that that behavior is wrong. We have to point out in a very sensitive way that it is a habit he'll have to break, a disease he'll have to be cured of, if he ever hopes to find his own personal happiness. He must acknowledge that morally and spiritually he wants to be a kinder and a gentler person both for his own good and the good of the woman he loves. I'll also try to get him into some kind of therapy that may include sensitivity training and anger management."

"And if all that fails?"

"We beat him like a redheaded stepchild," said Kent.

McGovern, who'd just wandered over from the dumper and caught only the tail end of the conversation, now weighed in with his considerable poundage on the subject at hand. He did not offer a joint this time, however. He only offered an observation.

"I saw a lot of that kind of abusive behavior growing up on the South Side of Chicago," said McGovern. "It was mostly because everybody was so poor and there really wasn't anything much to do. I remember as a kid, if you woke up on Christmas morning without an erection, you had nothing to play with all day."

CHAPTER TWENTY-EIGHT

ater that same evening I started to feel decidedly "crook," as Piers or Brennan might say. Ratso would probably say "fucked-up." I'm not sure what McGovern would say. He and Piers had been on the piss all evening. They'd gone out to the Monkey's Paw to plot some strategy about how to catch Tana Petrich and deliver her to the loft while avoiding assault and kidnapping charges if possible. When they returned that night I don't think they even noticed that my condition had deteriorated and, to be fair, I hardly noticed that theirs had as well. For his part, Kent Perkins had been last observed by me, before I'd retired to my sickroom, sitting stalwartly at my desk, tip-tip-tapping away at his little laptop, trying to run down background information on our mystery woman. There was something almost poignant about the big man who'd come all the way from California to sit patiently with his little laptop, working long into the lonely hours of the night to help his shivering, chattering, delirious friend resolve what was most likely a common domestic violence case, the very hardest to ever resolve, the least likely to ever, indeed, have a happy ending. Even as Ratso accompanied me into my bedroom, helped me into bed, pulled the comforters over me, and pulled a chair up for himself, I still had a lingering image in my mind of Kent Perkins, stoically sitting at the desk under the lamplight, ferreting for information and spiritual trivia from the Internet and PallTech, all to get the goods on a woman that only I had seen. He was doing this tedious, unrewarding, very likely futile labor, I knew, only for me. And, like Atticus Finch, I knew he would still be there in the morning.

So I lay there shivering in bed, watching Ratso eat a huge, cold roast beef sandwich, watching the cat watching Ratso with a visage of pure feline loathing, and wondering why it was so important to me to see this particular, rather singular affair to its conclusion. Was I trying to prove my own sanity? That was always an impossible proposition. Was I trying, as Kent presumably suspected, to "save" this woman? In moments of malarial lucidity, I realized with a thudding finality that it was not possible to save anybody in this life, not even myself. All you could ever hope to do was to lead people to the light, which, like Luke the Drifter, you couldn't even really see yourself. The malaria helped me in a way. I could watch myself walking on this lost highway of life. I could see that there was no light to see.

"Thank you for your company, Watson," I said. "How does it feel to know that there is no light?"

"There's always a light, Sherlock," said Ratso between bites. "It's waiting there for you at the end of the tunnel."

"That is death of which you speak, Watson! You're with a sick man in a sick room in a sick world and it is death of which you speak!"

"I missed a hockey game for this?" Ratso rather rhetorically asked the cat.

The cat, as I believe I told you, hated rhetorical questions. She hated Ratso even more. She was, in fact, so overwhelmed with hatred that, quite perversely, she suddenly chose to ignore Ratso completely. You can always learn something from a cat. If nothing else, you can learn to trust your instincts. If you don't, you could wind up a caricature of whoever you truly are, like a self-hating Jew driving a Mercedes.

"Watson," I said, through chattering teeth, "we know that the Internet is the work of Satan."

"Of course we do, Sherlock. Satan or Bill Gates. Same thing."

"So why are we allowing our private investigator friend from California to toil long into the dark night of the soul on the Internet to solve this case when we could just walk across the street like normal men in a normal world and knock on the door of the woman's third-floor apartment?"

"Because, Sherlock," said Ratso with what I detected to be a slight degree of irritation, "the woman's third-floor apartment doesn't exist."

"How do we know, Watson, that it doesn't exist?"

"Because the cops have already checked and it doesn't exist."

"Ah, Watson! But what if it's the cops who don't exist?"

"What if it's this conversation that doesn't exist?"

"Watson, Watson, Watson! Your whimsical nature is ever a cause for joy in this unhappy world!"

Having spoken these words, I was wracked with a ruthless, unforgiving bout of the shaking chills. The affliction was of such intensity and duration as to momentarily cause Ratso to stop eating his sandwich.

"Sherlock!" he cried. "Are you all right?"

"Do I look strange, Watson? By the way, those were Robert Louis Stevenson's last words to his wife just before he died. It was in his kitchen in Samoa. He didn't, of course, call his wife Watson. That would've never done. Now would it, Watson? However, the question remains: 'Do I look strange, Watson?'"

"You don't *look* too strange, Sherlock. You're *acting* a bit strange, but I think that's normal behavior for the course of the disease. Are you comfortable, Sherlock?"

"I make a living."

"Look, Sherlock. I want to talk to you about this investigation you and Kent are getting everybody involved in. I think it's good for you to be doing something while your doctor has confined you to the loft. Taking on a case like this may actually be therapeutic for you. It's certainly healthier for you than in the old days when all you used to do was hang around the loft taking cocaine and playing chess with the cat."

"What's wrong with taking cocaine and playing chess with the cat? She's a very conservative player, of course. Quite finicky. Sometimes she takes nine lives to make a move. The temperaments of cats are simply not well suited for chess, Watson, I'm afraid. Just as the temperaments of people are not well suited for living together in peace. I'm not criticizing the cat's game, mind you. She's a cautious player and a bad sport sometimes but if you don't pay attention she'll pounce on you every time. She could polish her end-game a bit. But really, Watson, so could we all."

"Fuck a bunch of cats and fuck a bunch of chess, Sherlock. All I'm saying is that while a bit of intellectual exercise may be therapeutic for you, an investigation of this nature may be harmful all around. It appears to be a common domestic abuse situation which even I, Watson, can diagnose. You've got Kent Perkins out there trying to prove to the world that California is the crime-solving capital of the universe. You've got Mick Brennan right now trying to focus that ridiculous spottah scope on an apartment that may not even be there. You've got Pete Myers taking time off from Myers of Keswick to feed what reminds me vaguely of the cast of *Bonanza*. Good sandwiches, of course. You've got Piers and McGovern attempting to work a supposed rescue mission that they probably couldn't even perform if they were sober. It's a fucking disaster, Sherlock. They're all just humoring you because you're ill. But just remember what your own chosen Dr. Watson tells you! It's a domestic violence case! It will end the way they always do! The man and the woman involved will end up loving each other and living happily ever after and they'll both wind up hating you!"

"Not as much as I hate you, Watson."

"I know you don't mean it. You're just delirious, Sherlock."

"Right."

"The question remains. Why have you become obsessed with

171

what is in reality a common circumstance of domestic violence?"

"Is it common, Watson? I think not. Malaria has caused me, or shall we say *permitted* me, to see reality in such a manner as never before. Watson, I tell you, I have not lost my powers of observation! Far from it, my dear friend! My powers have been honed to a degree of spiritual sharpness previously unknown in the foggy bathroom mirrors of men! A common circumstance of domestic violence! Ha! Ha! Ha! I'm afraid not, Watson! These are deep waters, indeed, Watson, as I'm sure our private investigator friend shall soon confirm."

It was a shot in the dark, of course. I knew Kent would undoubtedly come up with some background on Tana Petrich whether indeed she was alive or dead. Though the Internet existed, as far as I was concerned, to decide who was everybody's favorite *Star Trek* captain and to connect a short, fat, fifty-eight-year-old pedophile from New Jersey who was pretending to be a tall, young Norwegian chap with a vice cop in Omaha who was pretending to be a sixteen-year-old girl in San Diego, it was nonetheless not without some degree of functionality. I also knew that once Kent found some shard of peripheral information, he wouldn't be keeping it himself. And he realized I was a sick person in a sick room in a sick world and I wouldn't be popping out to check on him every five minutes. So it stood to reason he'd be making an appearance fairly shortly in my bedroom to announce some tissue of horseshit proclaiming his own abilities and the vital importance of the Internet. Therefore, it wasn't that much of a stretch that he'd soon be confirming my "deep waters, Watson" scenario. What was remarkable was that Kent's entrance occurred almost perfectly on cue.

"We're on to something big, boys!" Kent Perkins ejaculated, as his large Aryan form filled the small sickroom. "I've been busy reverse tracing the last known address of Tana Petrich. I'm looking for another woman of around the same age who might've blipped off the screen around the same time then resurfaced two or three years later. I can tell you one thing for sure. There's more here than meets the eye. Whoever took Tana's name went to a lot of trouble. There's a deep secret hidden here. Much deeper than just a woman changing her identity to avoid an abusive spouse."

During Kent's little speech, Ratso's eyes had become bigger than the saucers at the Mad Hatter's Tea Party. Now that a real private investigator had backed me up with the help of the Internet, he was once again a true believer in my cowboy intuition. His Doctor Watson had returned to form. He was ready to follow my Sherlock through the fires of hell.

"Justice rides a slow horse," Kent intoned, "but it always overtakes."

"Who said that?" asked Ratso.

"My great-grandfather," said Kent. "His name was Lorenzo Dow Posey and he was born in Winnfield, Louisiana. He was a Baptist circuit preacher and he married a Jewish girl from Philadelphia. When they moved back down South, as was rather common back then, she kept her religion a secret. On her deathbed she asked the whole family to gather around, she had something to tell them. To the family's abject horror, her last words were: 'Ah'm a Jeeeeeew!'"

"That means you're Jewish," said Ratso.

"I'm only Jewish from the waist up," said Kent. "But at least now I know why we only tithed $9.95."

"It's a curse," I said. "Like my father's old joke about the curse that comes with the Horwitz Diamond."

"What's the curse?" asked Kent.

"Horwitz," I said.

CHAPTER TWENTY-NINE

In the morning, Brennan came into my quarters with more good news. Pete Myers had brought me a British breakfast in bed, English breakfast tea, fried eggs, fried tomatoes, fried potatoes, fried toast, fried streaky bacon, and beans. Maybe I was off the lost highway and back on the road to recovery because everything tasted killer bee. Mick Brennan looked on approvingly for a moment, made a few solicitous remarks, then launched into his report.

"Top o' the mornin', ol' bean," said Brennan jovially. "Good to see you eating a proper English breakfast. I've photographed the girl."

"Fine, Watson, fine," I said. "Please give me the details."

"I don't have any details yet, mate. Film's being developed. But

I can tell you this. The girl's for real. She's not a figment of your fevered, malarial fantasies. Seen her meself, mate. First independent sighting, in fact. She lives! She walks! She takes off her clothes in front of her window!"

"Can you describe her, Watson?"

"Can I describe her? That spotter scope of your mate's leaves very little to the old imagination, if you know what I mean. She's a tasty bird. Great big Bristols. Large, wild, unpruned hedgerow."

"That may be a bit more information than we need, Watson."

"One more thing, mate. Let's jet this Watson shite, will you? Makes us sound like poofters. Anyway, Ratso's your Watson, innit he?"

"Any Watson in a storm, Watson."

"Bollocks!" said Brennan. "I'll let you know as soon as I have the prints."

"Fine, Watson, fine. Keep me in the picture, Watson. No pun intended."

"Hold on a tick, mate. I saw the bloke as well."

"You saw the bloke?"

"That's what I said, mate."

"Where was the bloke?"

"On top of the bird."

"You mean—"

"That's right, mate. They wasn't playin' Parcheesi."

"These are deep waters, Watson."

"Don't call me Watson."

With that word of admonition, Brennan goose-stepped back to his gaseous domain of chemicals in a darkroom somewhere, or possibly back to the spotter scope, or, quite conceivably, back to a pint of Guinness waiting to be poured. Everything was falling into place on this ship of fools we foolishly call the world. Now all I had to do was avoid the horse latitudes, the rocks, the sirens, the icebergs, the shipboard romances, the tyrannical captains, the pirates, the projectile vomiting caused by shipboard viruses, the projectile diarrhea caused by shipboard viruses, the projectile ennui caused by other shipboard passengers. And through the lonely, checkerboard night of the soul at sea, through another lighted porthole, could be seen the lithe form of the blithe woman making love to the dark form of the man who, very possibly, might soon murder her.

Later that day I emerged from my sick quarters for the first time in what seemed like decades. The loft looked like it'd been caught in the middle of a collision between a ship of fools and a garbage truck. The last man standing appeared to be Pete Myers, who was busily at work upon some arcane creation in the kitchen.

"What would you like, my lad?" he said. "Good to see you up and about. But you've got to keep putting food in you in order to sustain your body's energy level. So what's your fancy? Squeak and bubbles? Blood pudding? Spotted dick?"

"Nothing right now," I said. "I had a pomegranate on the New Delhi freight train. By the way, where the hell is everybody?"

"Well, Brennan's developing his prints from the spotter scope. Ratso's developing his Freudian theories about how investigating a bit of domestic violence may enhance the sex life of those who happen to view it vicariously. I'm developing a blister on my right hand from preparing the blood pudding. And Piers and McGovern are developing into two large pains in everybody's arse. They've been arguing apparently about your doctor at the hospital. McGovern wants to know if his name is really Dr. Pickaninny. He says if it's not, the name could be offensive to people of color and he wants to know why the rest of us continue to call him that. Piers tried to explain to McGovern that no one was calling anyone Pickaninny, that the man's real name is Dr. Skinnipipi and that McGovern is deaf and can't hear a sodding thing. McGovern insisted that he could hear people calling him Dr. Pickaninny and that it was alarmingly racist. Piers said that was good and then he called McGovern a pickaninny and that set the whole thing off again. Fortunately, they both appear to have taken a French leave at the moment and hopefully it will develop into a beautiful friendship."

"Where's Kent?" I asked, standing by the kitchen window and studying the fateful third-floor window across the street. The table was still there but the vase with the flowers was gone. Maybe she'd thrown it at the guy's head.

"Kent said he's developed a few promising leads. He said he was going out to do some old-fashioned legwork. He said he knew you'd be doing it yourself if you were able."

"Drink of my blood and eat of my body," I said.

"We do have the blood pudding," said Myers.

"We're going to have blood on Vandam Street if we don't resolve this matter soon, Watson."

Pete Myers did not answer. He merely looked at me and shook his head. Then he went to see if something was burning in the oven. I continued to watch the window and the building and Vandam Street, but all I saw were garbage trucks and pigeons and a few people walking rapidly, stiff-legged, leaning forward into the rain. Did I mention that it was raining? It always seemed to be raining on Vandam Street, and its gray shroud of shabbiness always seemed to remind me of Baker Street. This, however, was not a particularly singular phenomenon. When it's raining the whole world reminds you of Baker Street.

It wasn't too long after that that Kent Perkins came into the loft, shook the rain off his cowboy hat, poured himself a cup of Pete Myers's hot tea, and sat down in my chair by the desk. He continued to wear his wet clothes, but he was also wearing a big smile on his face.

"We're closin' in, Kink," he said. "Closin' in on the bad guys."

"You mean you think there may be more than one of them?"

"That's correct," he said, sipping the tea.

"Ah, Watson, what you modestly call your 'old fashioned leg-work' has confirmed a long-held opinion of my own. Pray tell me more, my dear, loyal, hard-working friend."

"I will," said Kent. "But first, don't you think you've carried this 'Watson' business a little too far?"

"What do you mean by that, Watson?"

"I mean that everybody can't be your Watson, nor should they. You're not being very polite to your friends and it's not healthy for all of us to be humoring you like this. It's kind of sad, really. At my firm in L.A., Allied Management Resources, I'd never treat my employees this condescendingly. I realize you were bit many years ago in the jungles of Borneo by a *Plasmodium*—"

"*Falciparum,* Watson. A *Plasmodium falciparum.*"

"Okay, so you were bit by a fucking mosquito. That doesn't give you a license to treat everybody like shit. And speaking of licenses, at least I have a PI's license and you certainly don't. What you have is a nasty little Christ complex and Sherlock is your Christ and all your supposed disciples are your Watsons. I don't like to see you this way, Kink, and, quite frankly, everybody's getting a little tired of it."

"What we have, Watson, is the country doctor, which is you, attempting to be the dime-store psychologist. Well, it won't fly into my airport, Watson! The game is afoot, Watson! We have work to do and I am afflicted with this accursed malady or, I assure you, I would do it myself! Now what have you discovered, Watson?"

"I've discovered that working with you can be pretty tedious."

"Watson, Watson, Watson. How very like you to bemoan the trivial frictions of day-to-day living when matters of mortal consequence pass by under our very window. How refreshingly human of you, Watson. But now we must turn our attentions to the affair at hand. What did you learn in your recent exploration of the living street?"

Kent's eyes looked tired. The big smile was now gone from his face. That was fine with me. I hadn't liked it that much anyway.

"Okay, Sherlock," he said rather grudgingly, "if that's how you want it. I did discover that the stories in the building across the street are numbered differently from this one. That building has a basement; this one doesn't. The basement counts as the first floor over there so what appears to be the third floor is actually the fourth. Are you with me?"

"Of course I'm with you, Watson. Where else would I be? Certainly you are to be congratulated. Your simple, pragmatic mind has found the answer to a problem that the very complexity of my approach had not resolved entirely and one, that I might add, has totally eluded the cops. I'm referring, of course, to the phenomenon of my looking one floor down across the street, yet the floor is numbered precisely the same as my own. Damned fine effort, Watson!"

"Thanks, uh, Sherlock."

"What else, Watson? What else have you for me?"

"I have this," said Kent, making a rather obscene gesture with his right hand.

"Ah, Watson, how like you to add a touch of levity to matters of such grave import! What else did you observe?"

"Well, I'll tell you. I did do a little bit of dumpster-diving behind the other building. It was loaded with all the usual shit you'd expect to find."

"Yes, yes, Watson. Garbage in, garbage out."

"Anyway, uh, Sherlock, I found this scrap of paper, which might hold some interest for your rapidly deteriorating brain."

"Far from it, Watson! Far from it! I see reality now like never before! It is, my dear friend, a heady experience that I recommend highly to all seekers of the truth! It is a strange and singular experience, Watson, into which lesser men might not deign to delve! Seeing reality as it really is, Watson, is like making eye contact with a unicorn!"

"Maybe you ought to make eye contact with this," he said, laying the paper down on the desk with a slight flourish.

I walked over to the desk, lifted Sherlock's cap, and removed a Cuban cigar. I lopped the butt off the cigar, and set fire to the tip with a kitchen match. I took a patient puff or two, blew a plume of purple smoke toward the building across the street, and, at last, picked up the piece of paper. It was a rent receipt for apartment number 412, dated the previous month. The name on the receipt was Tana Petrich.

Suddenly, my eyes began swimming and I could not see the words on the paper. I could not see Kent Perkins. All I could see was a man with a gun walking slowly toward me through the foggy Baker Street of the mind.

CHAPTER THIRTY

There's a difference between the cold sweats and the feverish chills, but you are never really able to make the distinction until you vaseline back and forth between the two of them about a hundred and seventeen times in the course of one night. One moment it felt cold enough for Jesus to piss icicles and the very next it was hot enough to pick up Hitler at the airport. If I was on the road to recovery, clearly I was taking a bit of a detour. This was enormously frustrating to me, as a detective and a person, because I felt more confidently than ever that we were very close to getting to the heart of the mystery of Tana Petrich.

I was not feeling all that well really, even as I stood in the brittle New York sunshine by the windows late the next morning. But feeling well, of course, is relative, and relative to the previous night I was feeling very well indeed. Maybe it was the sense that things were finally coming to more than a mere puppethead that was keeping me going. Sometimes that's all that keeps you goin', as my friend Hoover once wrote in a song. And I don't mean to be casting asparagus upon the puppethead. It was still my best friend in the world, though I didn't mention that to the Village Irregulars for fear they would be jealous or possibly even try to commit me to wig city. I just stood in the sunshine that there was and sipped some of Pete Myers's English breakfast tea and smiled a little twisted, serial killer's half-smile. At least I was ambulatory again. That was always preferable to ridin' through the desert on a horse with no legs.

"Care for a bit of brown sugar and cream with your tea, lad?" asked Pete Myers, rather solicitously, I thought.

"No," I said. "I'll take it brown, like my men."

"There's a lad," said Myers.

"How about taking some of this?" said Piers, holding up two bottles of Victoria Bitter. "Aussie piss beats limey tea any day."

"Where the hell are all the Americans?" I said, looking around the loft and finding four Village Irregulars missing. All I could see was the cat sitting in her rocking chair, smiling smugly, no doubt, at the absence of Ratso.

"Let me see," said Pete. "Brennan, who's lived here so long he might as well be an American, is in his darkroom somewhere developing the prints he shot through the spotter scope. McGovern has a story to file for the paper. Ratso, poor lad, has trekked down to Chinatown. Methinks he's had his fill of British cooking."

"I believe he may have taken a scunner to the spotted dick," said Piers.

"And Kent?" I asked.

Piers and Pete looked at each other rather conspiratorially, it seemed to me. Piers then took a mammoth slug of the VB, leaving only Pete to answer my question.

"Kent, who, by the way, seems like a very nice, loyal chap, is out pounding the pavement searching for clues for your investigation. Do you think, my lad, that it's wise to continue pursuing this effort?"

"Does it have to be wise?" I said, somewhat taken aback. "What if it's only the right thing to do?"

"Yes, but lad, *is* it the right thing to do? There were a number of cases that even your great British hero, Sherlock Holmes, decided at some fine point not to pursue. Possibly, we have no business meddling with these people across the street. Possibly, they're having their marital problems like any other couple and they've done nothing wrong toward any of us and they've committed no crime."

"The redback spider which lurks in outdoor shithouses in the bush," said Piers, "can kill a horse in a matter of minutes and a man in much less time. The male of the species, which is invariably eaten by the female, has a long, peculiar, corkscrew-shaped penis. This may be why he is invariably eaten by the female. Shall we investigate this case next? And what do you reckon we should do about the magpie having the largest testicles for its size of any creature in the entire avian kingdom, a condition often causing it to become rather aggressive and to take powerful pecks at passing people, not to mention other magpies? Shall we investigate this aggressive behavior, mate?"

I could see now that a large number of empty bottles of VB

were standing mutely on the counter. Myers looked sober as a judge and everyone else was gone and I knew the cat didn't drink.

"And then there's the singular case of the taipan snake," Piers was droning on. "Yes, mate, it's always a case of cold-blooded murder if you happen to be bitten by the taipan. You won't have time, mate, to upgrade your software. The taipan denatures the blood, breaking it down totally and instantaneously. The taipan can kill a horse in half a second. This is a real killer, mate. Shall we tail him relentlessly throughout the Antipodes?"

At this point, I could see Myers endeavoring to encourage Piers to pull his lips together, which was no small feat when Piers was on a roll. Piers and I probably talked more than anyone else I currently knew, the difference being that Piers could talk much louder than I could. In my weakened condition I saw no possible advantage in trying to defend my pursuit of the case, so I picked up the cat from the rocker, which always irritated her, and took her back into the bedroom with me.

Apparently there'd been some sort of mutiny in the ranks. Apparently there'd been some talking behind my back the previous night as I lay in fevered delirium, shouting salutations, I'm told, to deceased friends, and singing mournful verses of the American tune "The Ballad of Ira Hayes" and the Irish tune "The Ballad of Kevin Barry." I'm not sure which song is sadder and I didn't recall having sung either of them, but I did know that both men were heroes and they died on different sides of the pond, both tragically alone.

"The great King Kamehameha," I said to the cat, "was the man who conquered and united all the islands of Hawaii, except Kauai, into one great kingdom. He was a chief. He was a warrior. He was a king. And do you know what the name Kamehameha means?"

The cat, now struggling to get away from me and go into the other room, obviously did not know or care. She was never very big on island kingdoms. Too much water under the bridge of her nose.

"Kamehameha means 'the Lonely One,'" I said, holding the cat firmly in my arms as if she were my last friend in the world. "Sherlock Holmes was lonely, too. So was Sergeant Pepper. All men are lonely when they find the great work they love and believe in. This case is my work. This case is my brother. This case is the very thread by which I cling to sanity and to life itself!"

Sometime during the course of my little soliloquy the cat had managed to exit the room and Brennan had managed to gain ingress. Now he looked at me with the very same pity in his eyes that I had often observed in the traffic-light eyes of the cat.

"I won't bother you with processing details, mate, but we have very clear prints of the bloke and the treacle shot through the spotter scope. They're clean as the nose on your face. Well, maybe not your nose, mate. But they're brilliant, aren't they?"

Brennan proceeded to spread the prints out across the comforter and he wasn't wrong. They were brilliant, all right. It was the guy, all right. It was the girl, all right. And, God, if she didn't look just like Kacey.

"Watson," I shouted, holding the prints dramatically in the air, "these may be the pieces of the puzzle that allow us to finally break the case!"

"That's good, mate, because I almost broke my neck comin' up the stairs. Piers is passed out in the doorway."

"And this," I said, looking at the photo of the girl, "may be the piece of the puzzle that finally breaks my heart."

CHAPTER THIRTY-ONE

Looking back on events, I can now see, by the pale evanescent light of the celestial jukebox, that my friends, each in his own way, were trying to help me as best they knew how. Unfortunately, friendship is a skill that few of us truly master in the course of our lifetimes. With all of the tiresome projectile preaching and ruthless religious fervor of the past centuries and the current one, we still do not appear to grasp in our narrow, scattered, selfish and single-minded minds the simple message of one of the world's first great Jewish troublemakers, Jesus Christ.

Piers and Pete, I feel sure, were becoming convinced that humoring me along on a seemingly meritless adventure might only prolong my illness and bouts of irrationality. They probably thought that tough love might be the right approach to my problems. Brennan, I believe, was probably humoring me all the while, believing that one day I'd just snap out of it or else completely snap my wig and if it was the latter, he'd no doubt have to just keep humoring me forever. Many relationships and marriages exist in this fashion, each party determined to quietly humor the other, each party totally full of shit, each party determined to avoid at all costs the truth, each party eventually reduced to a bitter, constipated, humorless party of one. Well, I've always contended that friendship was overrated in the first place, while taking a Nixon in an Australian outback shithouse has always been underrated. Unless, of course, you get bit on the buttocks by a redback spider.

So much for how the three foreigners were attempting to handle the condition my condition was in. The Americans, for the most part, weren't that much more effective in dealing with it either. Ratso, who psychologically was well aware of the deterioration occurring within the once-rational brain of his beloved Sherlock, took the Jewish approach to dealing with his grief. He ate more food and most of it seemed to be Chinatown cuisine. I've noticed this phenomenon before in my life, Jews eating large quantities of Chinese food whenever their little world takes an unexpected turn, but I've never seen Chinese walking into delicatessens when things go awry. What does this tell us about the Jews and the Chinese? Do they need Jesus in their lives? I think not. One of the beautiful things about not believing in Jesus is that you rarely, if ever, misunderstand Him.

So Ratso wasn't much help or solace to me either, and McGovern, of course, did not realize half the time that my aberrant behaviors were being caused by malaria. He thought I was planning a trip to Bulgaria.

Then there was Kent, the true believer, the pilgrim who traveled east to help the Kinkster. Kent, like myself, understood what it meant to become involved with an investigation as tightly as the interwoven threads of life and death. Kent, like myself, knew how it felt to find yourself in the daunting position of being a mender of destinies. Kent, though mildly piqued with the Kinkster at the moment, I knew would rein in his frustrations and help bring the case to its logical conclusion. It wasn't long, in fact, after my having reflected upon these matters that Kent returned to the loft and more than justified my confidence in him.

"Okay, Inspector Clouseau," he quipped, "let's have a look at the photos."

Kent sat down at my desk in the chair he lately seemed to be occupying more frequently than myself. He turned on the desk lamp, which immediately drew the presence of the cat. Even with my warm houserobe over jeans and sweatshirt and mental hospital slippers, the loft seemed cold to me and the cat. Possibly, if we'd imbibed as much alcohol as some of the others, the loft and the world might seem a bit warmer. I, unlike the cat, had been known to take a drink, but the illness appeared to have put me off the piss, as Piers might say.

"Good Lord, Mick is really talented," said Kent. "These are the clearest photos I've ever seen shot under these conditions. I wish he lived in California."

"No you don't, mate," said Piers, who'd finally arisen from the hallway.

"The clarity is so good," Kent continued enthusiastically, "that I think we'll soon have the answer to the major question that's been bothering me."

"Which is?" asked Piers.

"Tell him, Kink," said Kent.

I found myself mildly flattered that Kent had passed the baton to me. It might also be a test, I realized, as to just how coherent and cogent were my current thought processes. I took a puff on the cigar I was smoking and took a crack at it gamely.

"I would say the major question that's been bothering you is the same one that's been bothering me," I said, stalling for time. I took another puff on the cigar and Kent made his traditional little California waving motion with his hand in front of his face as if the smoke was just too much for him. It irritated me to see this and I temporarily lost my train of thought.

"Well, mate," said Piers, turning toward me. "What is it that's troubling you two blokes?"

"The thing that's bothering me is that the girl is apparently using the identity of Tana Petrich, which I know because I saw the name on her driver's license. It was a fact I'd evidently repressed, one which Kent brought out later during hypnosis. Then we find that someone named Tana Petrich evidently died in 1991. So the nagging question, as I see it, is whether this girl is an imposter pretending to be Tana Petrich, or is she really Tana Petrich and, for reasons we don't as yet know, wants people to think that she's dead."

"Great minds think alike!" he said, jumping out of his chair to congratulate me. "That's exactly what I would have said. Either the death claim is fraudulent or the identity is fraudulent. Both cannot be real. One of them is phony and we're about to find out which one it is."

"We are?" I said.

"Of course," said Kent.

"How do you propose to do that?" I asked. A fraud perpetrated successfully for over ten years can often evade even the efforts of a major government task force.

"Easy," said Kent. "Call Rambam."

"Can't," I said. "He's somewhere in India right now, interviewing a dead swami. Can't even reach him on the shoe phone."

"Shit," said Kent. "This is the part of detective work that I hate. Rambam's a lone wolf. He's highly skilled in extralegal activities. I've now got twenty-six employees in my agency in L.A. and I have to be much more careful about how I do things. All private investigators are on both sides of the law, of course. Some are just more on both sides than others."

"Yeah, but Rambam only does that shit for me. We'll have to tackle the problem ourselves, Watson."

"I'm afraid so, um, Sherlock," said Kent. "I was hoping we could avoid having to do it ourselves. I was also hoping we could avoid this Sherlock-Watson shit."

"You're right on that last one, mate," said Piers.

"Ah, Watson," I said, "your earthy vernacular never fails to warm the coldest, most scientific soul. But I know you will not let me down at this grave moment, my dear friend. I am, as you well know, Watson, not a student of the modern technologies. I have made exhaustive studies of footprints and tobacco ashes, but this thing called the Internet, to which you've harnessed your very being, is beyond me, not to say beneath me. It is a fad of the moment. It shall pass and be forgotten, Watson. So-called modern technology will also pass and be forgotten. What is left, Watson, after all things impossible have been removed from the equation, will be only the possible as determined by the power of deductive reasoning. Now what do we do next, Watson?"

"Well, uh, Sherlock," said Kent. "We will do what Rambam probably would have done but we'll do it through the services of a second party. I will e-mail these photos to a friend who has access to these kinds of things and I will ask him to resolve the matter for us using any legal means possible. That last phrase is a sort of code, of course. It means, whatever it takes. We should have our answer very soon. Thanks to modern technology and the Internet, of course."

"Wonderful, Watson, wonderful! And if someone asks you later how you did it, what will you say?"

"I'll give them the same answer I always give them," said Kent.

"Which is?" asked Piers.

"I don't want to know," said Kent.

CHAPTER THIRTY-TWO

While Kent Perkins's mysterious friend tried for a computer match of Tana Petrich's photo, I paced the loft like a wind-up toy, smoking cigars and contemplating what our next move would be if the photos matched, or if they didn't match. Energy was coming back to me. Yet because of the stupid doctor's orders, I couldn't leave the loft. Not that there was much I could've done. I could, I suppose, have tried to stake out apartment number 412 across the street. I might still want to do that, I thought. But for the moment, the better strategy, it seemed, was to pace back and forth, smoke a cigar, listen to the pounding hooves of the lesbians above me, and wait for whatever results Kent's technological efforts might produce. It was a tedious job and I got to do it.

Some of the other Irregulars trickled back into the loft after a while, several of them expressing a renewed interest and confidence in the case the way Kent and his PallTech system appeared to be handling it. This got up my sleeve a bit until I thought of something Rambam had told me long ago. He'd called his weapon of choice in crime-solving "the hard-boiled computer." Reflecting upon it, I realized that Rambam quite possibly relied upon technology even more than Kent. It was simply that Rambam never used the computer or the Internet or PallTech or whatever the satanic system was around me. I only saw Rambam as a man of action. I never observed the sausages as they were being made.

Hell, I thought. The world was changing. Maybe every private investigator except me was now a technological junkie. I hoped not. As a rule of thumb I resisted change in all its nefarious forms, always remembering the wise words of Joseph Heller: "Every change is for the worse." Hell, I didn't even bother to change my underwear. I didn't, of course, wear any underwear. I preferred to go about commando-style. A little trick I'd picked up in the tropics. Probably about the same time I'd picked up malaria. Probably about the same time my penis had sloughed off in the jungle.

"There are only two databases for reliably obtaining photos," Kent was explaining to the small group of lookers-on gathered about the desk. "One is the federal passport database. That one's harder to get into than Fort Knox. The other one's the Department of Motor Vehicles database which every state has. What I haven't told you is that I've learned recently that Tana Petrich's last known address was in Florida."

"Why didn't you tell us that, mate?" asked Brennan.

"Because you didn't ask," said Kent.

He hadn't told me that information either, I realized. Some fucking Watson. Holding back vital details from Sherlock. Ah, well, I thought. Good help is hard to find these days.

"PallTech turned up the Florida address," Kent continued. "I happen to know a retired state trooper in Florida."

"Here I sit, strainin' my pooper," I chanted. "Tryin' to give birth to a Florida state trooper."

Kent chuckled politely. Several of the Village Irregulars glanced briefly at each other with worried expressions.

"What?" said McGovern. "Say again? Who took the pooper-scooper?"

"Troopah," said Ratso helpfully. "A Floridah state troopah."

"I heard you," said McGovern petulantly.

"Well, moving right along now," said Kent. "I'm now going to upload this beautiful photo of the girl known as Tana Petrich. I'll upload a digital image of Tana and my friend in Florida will have it along with my request for an identity match all within less than a second. That's pretty amazing if you think about it."

"So your friend gets the digital image," said Piers thoughtfully.

"Wrong tense," said Kent. "He's already got it."

"Pluperfect asshole," I muttered, but by now nobody was paying me any attention.

"So the former state troopah searches the Florida DMV database," said Ratso. "What's he actually looking for?"

"There aren't many Tana Petriches in this country," said Kent. "Maybe there's only one. PallTech tells us that she had a Florida driver's license. Kinky saw the driver's license and confirmed that the girl herself and her driver's license photo matched—"

"You're relyin' on his opinion, mate?" said Brennan, gesturing with a VB bottle in my direction.

"Hypnosis rarely lies," said Kent. "And PallTech never lies. PallTech has given us Tana's driver's license number, which I've also e-mailed to my friend. His job now is to find another photo of Tana and then we'll know if Tana's really Tana."

There were nods of understanding and agreement from most of the Village Irregulars. Pete Myers interrupted me in midpace to give me a hot steaming cup of Ulong Blue Dong or whatever limey tea is supposed to be served at 1:17 p.m. to a man convalescing from malaria. I sipped the tea. I puffed a bit on the cigar.

"What do we do now, mate?" asked Brennan.

"Now," said Kent, "comes the hard part. We wait."

It was kind of a funny picture actually. Six men standing around like village idiots, occasionally peering over the shoulder of a large blond-haired man sitting at a desk essentially doing nothing. They looked for all the world like seven city workers standing around watching a machine. Maybe, I thought, the glorious, wonderful, satanic, fucking technological revolution hasn't come as far as people would like to think.

Time passes slowly when you're waiting for a response from a machine that supposedly operates at the speed of light. There was time for three or four hearty rounds of drinking by all of the Village Irregulars except for Kent. There was time for McGovern to break into his stash and pass around another kingsize joint of his "wheelchair weed." There was time for McGovern to follow up this particular amusement by patronizingly inquiring about my general state of health. I told him it was incredible to me that after all this time my body and mind still often seemed in the grip of malaria. He did his usual, maddening, "Say again?" routine and when I ignored it, he wanted to know why I was planning a trip to Bavaria.

Perhaps it was because Kent was trying to maintain the interest of his crowd that he launched into a series of Hollywood celebrity stories, mostly dealing with Frank Sinatra and Dean Martin. He did, of course, have somewhat of an insider's knowledge of these men because his wife, Ruth Buzzi, was much adored by both of them. Frank regarded her as his daughter and Dean wanted her on every Dean Martin Roast. The Village Irregulars, like almost all of us, were suckers for firsthand Hollywood celebrity stories. While Kent's little laptop hummed hopefully, the little group stood around him listening to his tinseltown tales with their eyes popping and their jaws hanging open. Much of this reaction, of course, could have been attributable to the wheelchair weed. As I paced back and forth across the long, cold living room of the loft, I picked up little snippets of conversation. It was interesting. It was kind of like the atmosphere you might find on a stakeout. Some of the most interesting, freewheeling conversations I'd ever had had occurred when I'd been on stakeouts with Rambam.

"Yeah, I currently own Dean Martin's old Rolls-Royce," Kent was saying. "It's tan and sand. Beautiful car."

"How much did it cost?" asked Ratso.

"Let's just say," said Kent, "it was an offer I couldn't refuse."

"Ever had one of Frank's cars, mate?" asked Brennan.

"No," said Kent. "But Frank really was a loyal, classy guy in his own way—if you were his friend, of course, or maybe just somebody in need of his help. Every year, in fact, he'd call Ruthie on her birthday. He'd say: 'Let me speak to Ruthie.' And I'd say: 'Who's calling?' And then he'd say: 'Frank.' Then I'd say: 'Frank who?' And then there'd always be a long pause. Then he'd say in a low, growling voice you knew not to mess with: 'Frank Sinatra.' And I'd say: 'Just one second, Mr. Sinatra.'"

"Yes," said Piers. "And speaking of Hollywood stories, Ted Mann called me about the almost-famous star of a recent TV series. He's a pretty good actor, apparently, but he'd been doing a lot of marching powder in his trailer and running prostitutes in and out and making about six hundred people on the set miserable. Finally, the guy got carried away one day and beat up one of the girls in his trailer. The next day, the network canceled the show. So a few days later, he comes in to see the producer and says he's sorry and wants to know if his behavior might have had anything to do with the cancellation. The producer looks at him and says: 'Slap a ho. No mo' show.'"

"Then there was the time," said McGovern, "many years ago, when Albert Einstein went to visit his friend Charlie Chaplin in Hollywood. Chaplin took Einstein with him to his favorite restaurant. When they got out of the car there was a crowd gathering around. So Einstein turns to Chaplin and says: 'Why are those people pointing at us?'"

"Why is Ratso pointing at Sherlock Holmes?" I asked. For, indeed, Ratso appeared to be pointing at the bust of Sherlock on my desk.

"I'm not pointing at Sherlock," said Ratso. "Look at the screen."

The entire group now crowded around the desk where Kent's little laptop stood in the spotlight. I walked over too, but the assembled multitudes prevented me from even seeing the desk.

"Does the photo look like Tana?" I asked nobody in particular. "Is the girl a brunette?"

"She's a brunette, all right, mate," said Brennan. "Have a look."

Brennan pushed McGovern and Piers out of the way as if they were sides of beef. Like a modern-day Moses he parted the Red Sea for me, not to the Promised Land or the throne of Jesus, but to the laptop of Kent Perkins. The image of the real Tana Petrich filled the little screen. She was a brunette. She was also a jovial-looking, chubby black woman who bore an almost eerie resemblance to a young Aunt Jemima.

"She's right off the pancake carton," said Kent. "You know what this means?"

"I hope it means that Aunt Jemima's coming to cook us some real breakfast," said Ratso, "instead of fucking baked tomatoes and beans and fried eggs on top of everything and spotted dick—"

"Cook it yourself," said Pete Myers, and, in an unusual display of emotion, he threw a large spatula, narrowly missing Ratso's head.

"It means," said Kent, oblivious to the mindless activity behind him, "that our Tana Petrich is a little imposter. And I think she's hiding a nasty little secret."

"And what of Aunt Jemima?" asked Piers.

"She's dead, of course," said Kent.

"You lives by the watermelon," I said, "you dies by the watermelon."

"That statement is rather alarmingly racist," said McGovern.

"Kiiinnnnnk," said Kent.

"I'm not a racist," I said. "I'm just trying to save a soul some pain."

Chapter Thirty-three

So what's our next amusement?" said Piers, early that evening as a chill wind blew recklessly down Vandam Street. I'd been huddling at the desk with Kent for the better part of two hours, bracing myself with Pete Myers's hot tea, and also bracing myself for what I strongly suspected was the imminent end-game.

"Our next amusement," I said, "will no doubt demonstrate to us all what a funny, sick world we really live in."

In spite of the chill wind, I was feeling fairly feverish now and I could almost see Piers's intelligent eyes calculating not unkindly my relative sanity at the moment. That was probably why I motioned for Kent to explain the plan the two of us had hammered out. Kent had been my eyes and my legs. Now he could speak with my very voice. Malaria had brought reality to my life. It was the reality of a dreamer who now realized, perhaps a little too late in the game, that he was impotent when it came to holding on to his dreams. I could no more save the girl who called herself Tana than I could save myself. Or the girl I used to know.

"It's more than just a hunch now," said Kent. "It's more than just some domestic abuse going on here, not to make light of domestic abuse. But there's something else at play. This girl has another name out there somewhere. She has a reason for going to all the trouble of assuming a false identity. When you see enough of this kind of thing you develop an internal alarm system. Lots of people carry fake IDs, kids have learned to falsify their driver's licenses so they can buy liquor. It's often no big thing. But this one feels different. For one thing, they usually cross-reference credit bureau records with the death index these days. We know Tana's paying the rent for that apartment across the street and we know she's lived there a long time."

"How do we know that?" asked Ratso.

"Because if she'd tried to rent the place in the recent past they'd have known she was dead. So she's probably continued to maintain this false identity for over ten years. Why? Why would she go to the trouble? Why would she take the risk?"

Ratso and Piers pondered the question. McGovern was asleep on the couch. Brennan was standing near the window, making minute adjustments on the spotter scope. As I watched him, he suddenly let out a shriek that sounded like it came all the way from Lower Baboon's Asshole.

"Treacle ahoy!" shouted Brennan. "Just off the starboard bow, maties!"

Suddenly, I was wide awake. McGovern was wide awake. The whole place was as active as a recently-stepped-in ant hill. There were of course, differing reasons for this behavior.

"Crikey! The bird's just getting out of the shower!" shouted Mick. "She's wearing nothing but a little plastic cap on her head!"

"Let me have a look!" shouted Ratso, elbowing his way through the crowd. "I'm getting more interested in the investigation."

"What else do you see?" I asked Mick.

"Not much," said Brennan. "Other than the bird, of course. This spotter scope is brilliant! Now she's turning around to towel off her legs! Hey, Kinkster! I thought you said this place didn't have a view!"

"Is the guy there?" Kent asked.

"No sign of him," said Brennan.

"Anything else happening in the apartment?" I asked.

"Nothing much. Everything looks about the same. There's a suitcase on the bed. Now she's applying some kind of lotion to her body—"

Kent and I exchanged a hurried glance. It looked like the last train was about to leave Gun Hill. If we were going to make a move with the woman who called herself Tana Petrich, it would have to be pretty damn quick. Otherwise, our bird would have flown.

"The old suitcase on the bed trick," said Kent. "I've got to interview this girl before she flies the coop."

"Can we get in the building?" I asked.

"It's a lot more secure than this one, I can tell you that," said Kent. "I've already done it. But there's no listing for her apartment number and we don't know when the guy's coming back and besides, I don't want to panic her."

205

"I guess they don't have puppetheads over there," said Ratso.

"Doubtful, mate," said Piers.

"Well, Watson," I said, turning to Kent. "In this time of my infirmity, I must rely upon your astute judgment even more than usual."

"Let's call her," he said.

"There's one little problem with that plan," said Ratso. "Not only do we not know her real name, we don't even have her telephone number."

"If she's hidden her true identity for more than ten years now," said Piers, "it's highly unlikely that it'll be listed in directory assistance."

"Worth a try," said Kent.

While I lit a cigar and Ratso checked the refrigerator, Kent tried information. There was no Tana Petrich.

"If at first you don't succeed," said Kent, "ask for a supervisor."

"A wise adage, Watson," I said. "I'll have Mrs. Hudson stitch it on a pillow for us."

But Kent Perkins was already on a cell phone, waiting for the supervisor to come on the line. Piers and I leaned our elbows on the kitchen counter and watched him with bemusement. Pete had gone out for more provisions, or "tucker," as Piers invariably called it. And as for Ratso and McGovern? They were aiding the investigation by helping Mick Brennan monitor the action across the way through the spotter scope.

"What I'm about to do I haven't done in twenty years," said Kent, covering the cell phone with his hand. "Not since I worked for a crooked PI in L.A. But something tells me the situation calls for it. Tana's life might be in danger. She may be being held against her wishes. It's even possible—Yes, Ms. Dsouza, this is Detective Sergeant Johnny Dark from the Airport Police, badge number 7492, calling with a police emergency. Yes. The mobile command post at Kennedy. I've tried to reach the security office. There's a problem. You're the backup number on my log. Yes. I need the number of a Tana Petrich, 198 Vandam Street, apartment 412."

As Kent waited, I noticed fine beads of sweat breaking out on his brow. This was obviously something that pained him to do. He was a pilgrim, all right, I thought. He still had that thing they used to call a conscience.

"Okay, that's 586-4275. Thank you, Ms. Dsouza." Kent flipped the cell phone closed and wiped the sweat from his forehead. "I guess I needed the practice," he said

"What's next?" asked Ratso.

"Next comes the hard part," said Kent.

CHAPTER THIRTY-FOUR

Matlock had nothing on Kent Perkins when it came to country charm. Add to that Kent's father confessor–good cop
approach, and it was almost like providing a roadmap to a lost
soul. But first, of course, we had to get the lost soul to agree to
cross the street, climb four flights of stairs, step over a few errant
cat turds and beer bottles, and be interviewed by Kent Perkins. It
was not going to be an easy task to convince someone to follow
this course of action. Particularly, I thought, if she already had her
suitcase on the bed.

I was just emerging from the dumper, attending to some early
evening ablutions, when I noticed that the end-game had already
begun. I would have preferred to have been more actively
involved in the end-game, but sometimes that's not the card life

deals you. Sometimes you just have to learn how to play a poor hand well.

"I'm going to call the girl," said Kent, as he stood by the windows with his cell phone and gazed purposefully across Vandam Street. "Mick! Spotter scope down!"

"Aye, aye, mate," said Brennan, as he began quickly disassembling the tripod.

"Oy, oy, mate is more like it," said Piers. "This little adventure could turn into a real disaster. You have a jealous, abusive psycho with a gun living right across the way, and now you're luring his equally unstable sheila over here. Remember, Kinkster, the rest of us can always leave. You've been grounded by Dr. Skinnipipi."

"Fuck Dr. Skinnipipi," I said, "and the proctoscope he rode in on."

"The whole thing is academic anyway," said Ratso. "Today, even if you can make yourself heard, no one believes what you tell 'em."

"What?" said McGovern. "Say again? You believe the cat turds are *smellin'*?"

"No, McGovern," I said. "We were just discussing the voyages of *Magellan*."

"I can hear you," said McGovern petulantly. "You don't have to shout."

"What he was really saying," said Piers, with an almost aboriginal insight, "is that the girl may be a dangerous *felon*."

"Those may well be," said Kent Perkins, "the truest words we'll hear all night."

It's possible, of course, in this funny old world we live in, for someone to be the bad guy *and* the good guy at the same time. Or the good girl and the bad girl. I knew I was empathizing a bit too heavily with the woman who called herself Tana Petrich. And when you empathize with someone it severely impedes your abilities to think rationally, much less reason deductively. Empathizing with someone, I reflected, was almost as bad as loving them.

"My name is Kent Perkins and I know your name is not Tana Petrich," said Kent into a cell phone seemingly smaller than a magpie's testicle.

The big man with the small phone, standing casually by the window as if he were talking to a friend, was a portrait of relaxed confidence. It was almost like he was fishing. He'd hooked the fish when she'd picked up the phone. One false word or reckless nuance and we all knew he'd lose her.

"I'm not a cop or I'd be over there kicking in your door with an arrest warrant and handcuffs right now. Believe it or not, I'm interested in helping you."

I think at that moment every one of us believed that Kent Perkins could and would help the girl. Even those cynics who thought he was doing what he was doing out of friendship for me or out of some misguided stratagem to bring me out of my malaise were impressed with his cool demeanor and his humanity.

"I know you're in trouble, but there is a way out. But you've got to meet me halfway. I believe I have some information that might just save your life."

For a telephone conversation of this nature, this was already a long one. It was beginning to look like Kent might, indeed, reel her in. From across the room, McGovern was already giving him an enthusiastic thumbs-up, a gesture that was as well-intentioned as it was poorly timed. I'm not sure Kent even saw it. I'm not sure he saw anything during the torturous course of that call except a last chance to help a lost soul.

Certainly, the words themselves were well-chosen and crucial. But it was the voice itself, simple, sincere, urgent, charitable, that, I believe, made the difference. And, of course, it was high drama. Kent seemed to know that everything was riding on every word. This was no longer just another case. This was no longer a matter of routine, of going through the motions. Maybe it really was nothing more than a common case of domestic abuse, but it was clear that Kent had put his heart into it. He was talking her down from the bridge. And though the spotter scope was now turned away from the window, and the night was dark, and we could no longer see the girl, we could almost feel her glancing at the suitcase on the bed. The conversation continued for a few more moments, then, with a breathtaking suddenness, it reached its conclusion.

"Okay," said Kent. "I'll meet you in thirty minutes on the street. Now dry off that big, beautiful vagina of yours and get yourself downstairs, honey."

The small audience in the loft received Kent's closing remarks in stunned silence. For a long moment, no one said a word and only the puppethead was smiling. Then Kent gave a small shrug and a somewhat sheepish smile.

"Just seeing if you were paying attention," he said. "I'd already hung up."

CHAPTER THIRTY-FIVE

I relapsed very badly that evening. Maybe it's just what happens when you have malaria. Maybe it was brought on by my over-identification with my field of study. Maybe it was the sheer karmic intensity of Kent trying to reel in the big one. Maybe it was none of the above. None of the ceilings or lesbians or stars. All I really remember before getting my ticket punched to Neverland was Kent asking everybody to please leave the loft for a while so he could interview the girl. The next thing I remember was Ratso tucking me into bed like a little child and saying he'd come back later to check on me.

There wasn't that much to check really. My mind seemed to be floating somewhere over the Mexican-Israeli border. I was having the kind of vivid, twisted, opiumlike, technicolor dreams that normal people never have. I was fucking a girl who couldn't remember where she was when JFK was assassinated because she wouldn't be born for two more decades. She thought JFK was an airport, RFK was a football stadium, and Martin Luther King was a street running through her town. The only common ground we ever found was on her futon. She'd never heard of Jack Benny, Humphrey Bogart, or Abbie Hoffman, but she thought Hitler may have been a punk band in the early eighties. We got along pretty well because I didn't remember much either. All in all, it wasn't a bad dream.

When I woke up I didn't know where I was or what time it was. I only knew that I was sporting a monstro erection and drowning in an ocean of sweat. Then I heard the two voices in the living room. A man and a woman. The man, I quickly realized, was Kent Perkins. The woman, I knew in my gut, was the woman who called herself Tana Petrich. The same instincts that told the cat to hate Ratso told me that the next amusement was going to be a tragedy.

"Nobody's going to grab you or hold you here, young lady," said Kent. "Nobody's going to force you to stay here to meet with me. That's why I've put your chair closer to the door."

"Okay," she said, rather tentatively.

"I know you're here tonight because you're worried about what I might know. Well, it's not my job here to tell you about yourself. It's my job here to see if we can help you get into a safer place, out of the bad situation you're in."

"But I'm—"

"I know you're in trouble. I've been conducting an ongoing investigation. I'm working for someone who will remain nameless

214

for now, for reasons which I'll explain later. I'm not a cop. I'm not here to hurt you in any way. In fact, I would like to help you."

"Thanks, but—"

"You're a person who is very, very afraid, and I understand that."

"Do you?"

"I know you're in a desperate situation with the man across the street."

"I think I'd—"

"Better go? That's fine. But I have evidence that could get the police involved. I don't want them handling this. I think it might be in your better interest to leave them out of it."

"All right."

"You know, you've got to be the one to help yourself here. I can bring some suggestions to the table, but you've got to be the one to take real action to change things. That guy has beaten you nearly to death a few times and now he's waving a gun around. Frankly, I don't think your life expectancy's too long at 198 Vandam. I've been an investigator for a long, long time and I've seen situations like yours before. Nobody ever de-escalates violence on his own. It just gets worse. So, you see, you're free to leave, but if you do, you'll never know whether we might've been able to help you."

"I'm listening."

"If you're ready to get out of that bad situation over there, then we need to talk. My friends and I will help you on the condition that you level with us. You have to be sincere with us in order to be true to yourself. And I have to measure your sincerity very carefully to determine whether you're really worthy of our efforts. We're talking major rescue endeavor here, with obviously some danger in this for us, too, right?"

"Right. He won't stop at anything."

"Okay. I'm ready to continue if you are. I have to measure your sincerity now. Trouble is, sincerity is an intangible thing, right?"

"Right."

"So, to measure an intangible like sincerity, we have to measure the closest almost-tangible thing—sincerity's closest cousin—and that's honesty. Do you understand and agree with that?"

"Yes."

"So measuring honesty means asking some questions I already know the answers to. This gives me a clear reading of your level of honesty. I can then translate that to imply just how sincere you are, understand?"

"Yes."

"Let's start with the first page of this investigative manual. Research reveals you are not the person you've been claiming to be. Tana Petrich is not your real name. Honesty test question number one: Say your real name."

"Is that whole file on me?"

"This whole file is my investigative manual, which contains all the information I've been able to amass about you since I started this investigation. I need to use this material to determine whether you are being truthful, honest, and sincere tonight."

"Give me my first initial. Just to show me you really know who I am. Then I'll tell you."

"I could do that except that I need for you to be one hundred percent honest. Giving you the first initial would mean that you're testing me, not the other way around. You see, for a very good reason, for your own safety and out of real concern for your well-being, I'm the one testing you. It takes a more honest person to answer a question truthfully without prompting like that. If you think you're here to test me, then you can just hit the door. Go ahead. Walk out of here and turn your back on all this effort. It's your life, young lady. People getting together and trying to help a total stranger in the middle of New York City may seem too weird to grasp. I understand that. It's okay. Just leave."

Confined to my bed like a shut-in, I found myself inextricably caught up in this little drama, like an old-time radio soap opera of the mind. Would the girl leave? Would she stay? Was Kent selling the door too aggressively? Tune in next week to find out.

"Okay, but this better not be a trick," she said. "My name is Sarah."

"Great start," said Kent enthusiastically. "You're doing great! Shake my hand, Sarah. I know that was difficult."

In my shivering, frazzled mind I could see Kent Perkins, a big Texas smile on his face, extending a warm hand of friendship to the troubled girl. With talent like that, I thought, he could have made millions as a motivational speaker for large California corporations. I suspected, though, that he knew God didn't like motivational speakers or large California corporations. That was probably why Kent Perkins, instead, had chosen to be a mender of destinies.

"Sarah," he said. "Now say your last name."

217

"Are you sure you're not the police?"

"That's a long name," said Kent. I could hear him getting up out of his chair, walking over to the girl. "Look at this, Sarah. This is my ID. Right here over my name are the words 'Private Investigator,' and here on the back of the card it says, 'Not affiliated with any law enforcement agency.' It says that for a reason, Sarah. I couldn't carry this if I was a cop."

"Okay. It's Sarah Kenter. That's Zarah with a 'Z,' though it's pronounced the regular way."

"Zarah, that took courage, and I appreciate that very much. I *had* been pronouncing your name wrong. Thanks for straightening me out. Now, Zarah, you have to tell me your date of birth. Not Tana Petrich's, but Zarah Kenter's."

"Three twenty-three seventy-seven."

"Very good, Zarah. Okay. And now one of the toughest questions. What are you running from?"

"You know who I am, so you obviously know about the Brinks robbery in California."

"Yes, I sure do."

"Well, they told me nobody'd get hurt. I was horrified when Ben—"

"Ben who?"

"Let's call him Ben Felch."

"Okay. Ben Felch. Go ahead."

"When Ben started shooting. I was an assistant to a Brinks dispatcher. I could've stopped it. Now we're wanted for murder and interstate flight and robbery and, hell, I don't know what else."

"That wasn't your first caper, was it, Zarah?"

"If you've really done your research, you know the answer to that, Mr. Perkins."

"Call me Kent."

"Kent. I was recruited because I was clean enough to pass the background and get hired at Brinks. I'd only worked in dispatching for a few months before the holdup."

"Tell me about this Ben Felch. Where'd you meet him?"

"He was working for my dad in a work-release program out of the California Department of Corrections. My family's in the flower business and dad hired him under a government grant. He was supposed to be working in the greenhouse, taking care of the plants. I found him attractive. I was just sixteen and ready to experience life a lot more than my parents wanted. They would've died if they'd known what we were doing. I'd never been with a real man before and I guess I thought I was in love. He got me kind of addicted to him, you know? We did pot, did a few other drugs, and before long I was pretty strung out. He grew enough marijuana back there, out of sight, to bankroll the Brinks operation. One day he showed me a wad of twenties and said, 'Let's get out of here.'"

Zarah Kenter went on to pour her heart out, not without a few tears, to Kent Perkins, and, though she didn't know it, to me as well. A nightmare decade of abuse, blackmail, hopelessness, and despair. I heard Kent encouraging her to leave Felch now, leave New York immediately. He would help her get out. He had a friend who had a ranch in Texas. He'd once safely hidden Abbie Hoffman there when the feds were searching for him.

"Who's Abbie Hoffman?" she asked.

"Abbie Hoffman was many things," said Kent. "One of them was a federal fugitive, not unlike yourself."

"Did he get away?" she wanted to know.

"Not really," said Kent.

Not really, I thought. Only a little piece of him got away. Like Joan of Arc, or Davy Crockett, or Anne Frank, or Che Guevara, or Jesus Christ. Only a little piece of the puzzle ever gets away. No point in telling the poor kid now. Hell, I reckoned, we're all prisoners of Vandam Street. Zarah Kenter certainly was. And here I lay in my narrow, monastic, Father Damien–like bed, confined to the loft like Nero Wolfe, confined by his gargantuan, sedentary buttocks to his brownstone. Like Sherlock Holmes on a cocaine binge, self-imprisoned in his lonely flat on Baker Street with only the fog for a friend. Yes, Zarah, your little friends are full of shit. No matter what our ZIP code happens to be in this world, one way or another, we're all prisoners of Vandam Street.

I heard her tell Kent that she believed that the abusive, murderous thug she called Ben Felch would be out of town for another day or two. That would give her a little time, she said. She had a few things she had to do before she got back to Kent. Kent didn't like it. He wanted her to go with him, get the suitcase off the bed, and leave New York now. He'd take her to the airport, buy her a ticket to Texas. As a private investigator who'd finally ferreted out the truth, he was willing to give her a spiritual pass and she didn't even know it. Maybe he'd "sold the door" too well.

CHAPTER THIRTY-SIX

Every story has to end and every friend has to go back to California. It was two days later, on a cold, sun-splattered morning. Much improved, I was standing in the kitchen of the loft next to Pete Myers, watching the maddeningly slow process by which he brewed his special British tea. I'd become fairly addicted to it by this time, so there was nothing to do but watch and wait. Kent Perkins was taking a much-needed nap on the couch. He was still waiting to hear from Zarah Kenter. He still believed she was going to call. As for myself, I wasn't so sure. It was the basic difference between a dog and a cat, I thought, between a Christian and a Jew. Kent, like an intelligent, loyal dog, believed in people, believed in fairies, believed in happy Hollywood endings. He even believed that California was not a towaway zone. The cat's eyes and my eyes were the same eyes; we'd already seen far too many things to believe in any of them.

Kent said he had done all he could do. He'd given Zarah his card before she'd left, telling her he was waiting in the full-crouch position to hear from her. It was a 1–800 number and they'd plug her right through to him twenty-four hours a day. He figured she'd call when she was ready. In the meantime, there were millions of other Zarahs out there in the cold, cruel world who might be in need of his help. Kent planned to take the red-eye back to L.A. late that night.

For my part, I'd been improving so steadily that most of the Irregulars had already gone their merry way. Piers was en route to Australia to continue a lifetime of research into the relative weight of the testicles of the magpie. The research, of course, is not without some personal risk to Piers's person, since the Australian magpie is a very aggressive bird known to dive-bomb and attack passing schoolchildren, nature enthusiasts, and pluperfect assholes. Piers, a rather aggressive man with rather large testicles of his own, I felt sure would be a perfect match for the pesky, pernicious, pusillanimous bird.

McGovern was back at his place on Jane Street. Like all the rest of us, he was probably hearing what he wanted to hear. Despite all the tiresome shouting, enunciating, and repeating ad nauseam, however, I missed McGovern. And I missed Piers. I even missed Brennan, who was off on assignment, I believe, to an important shoot in Upper Baboon's Asshole. Pete Myers had also announced his departure that afternoon. I would miss Pete and his cooking. Some time after he'd gone I noticed a great many tea bags that he'd thoughtfully left behind in the sands of time.

Unfortunately, I would not get the chance to miss Ratso. He wasn't leaving, he said, until he was certain there'd be no more relapses. This was, of course, bad news for the cat, but she took it in stride. Ratso did come in handy later that night, driving Kent to the airport. For one brief, shining moment the cat and I were totally alone. Then, of course, faithful as a German train schedule, Ratso returned.

Like so many sacred stray dogs and cats, people come in and go out of your life, and the ones that are the farthest away sometimes seem to be the closest to your heart. Your home is your castle until one day, quite inexplicably, it becomes your prison. One day you see a girl who reminds you of another girl who reminds you why you're still alone. One day your friend Ratso tells you that he's been studying the medical literature and he has learned that a malarial relapse virtually guarantees that you will never get syphilis. And so, I tell him, something positive *has* come out of all of this after all.

Later that night, while Ratso and I were in the midst of a mildly unpleasant altercation regarding a renewed, rather deliberative dumping campaign on the part of the cat, I happened to glance out the window and notice several large cardboard boxes on the sidewalk in front of 198 Vandam Street. I didn't think anything of it at the time. Still later that night, with Ratso crashed on the couch and the cat sleeping soundly on my pillow, I got up to check the refrigerator, figuring that maybe there was a little leftover spotted dick or something.

I made myself a cold roast beef sandwich and was preparing to have a little conversation with the puppethead, when I decided to check out the window and see how the cardboard boxes were doing. They seemed to be getting along fairly well. Not too much flap. I was lighting a cigar when I saw the man known as Ben Felch come out of the building with a suitcase, hail a taxicab, and disappear into the night. It happened so suddenly it almost seemed like a dream. The man was certainly taking a lot of business trips. Three nights before, Zarah had told Kent he'd been gone on another one.

I looked up at Zarah's window across the street. It was dark. Of course almost every window on Vandam was dark. It was three o'clock in the morning. There was nothing I could do really, and there was no reason to do it. Felch would come back. He'd beat up Zarah again. She'd probably tell people she'd fallen down the stairs. This kind of chronic domestic violence went on all over the world. It was as predictable and as unpreventable as the tides or the phases of the moon. Yet there was no moon that night. I don't know about the tides, but I tossed and turned and I didn't get to sleep until just before dawn.

I got up late the next morning. Ratso was having an espresso. I was having a cigar and a cup of English breakfast tea. The cat was having Carved Salmon in Gravy. I gazed down at Vandam Street and saw a homeless woman going through the two cardboard boxes. She had most of their former contents scattered out along the sidewalk. The boxes, apparently, had contained women's clothing. There were shoes. There was lingerie. There were pants and blouses and tops. There was one nice blue dress.

CHAPTER THIRTY-SEVEN

It took the better part of a week for me to convince the cops to check apartment 412 across the street. They had a record of the 911 call and the police report of that incident and they were not eager to get burned again listening to the rantings and wild imaginings of a malaria patient. When they finally did check the apartment, an old lady named Mrs. Finkelstein was living there with her dog Sparky. She had just moved in recently, she told the cops. Other than that, she was not very friendly or forthcoming with them. The cops, in turn, were not very friendly or forthcoming with me.

Apartments rent fast in New York. Your apartment can be rented before you even know you're dead. But not everything in New York moves as fast as an apartment. Though I was convinced that a crime had occurred, the cops weren't buying any. They refused to seriously consider getting a search warrant to search the apartment or the building. It was all circumstantial, they said. All a malarial fantasy. People move out of the city every day, leaving old clothes behind for homeless people to pore over on the sidewalk. Forget about it, they said. There's not enough there to do anything with.

But they were wrong. There was a lot there. Trouble was, it was all in my head and in my heart. And as many months went by, that was where it stayed. Maybe it was because Zarah had been about the same age as Kacey when I'd first seen her long ago across a crowded room. Maybe it was because malaria had helped me see reality, and reality, I believed, was that Ben Felch had murdered Zarah and gotten away with it. Maybe it was just personal and professional pride; I hadn't come this far to be just another guest voice on *The Simpsons*. Whatever it was I believed, however, nobody wanted to hear it. Even Kent Perkins wasn't sure. A lot of things could've happened, he told me one night on the phone. That's true, I said, but only one of them did. The only reason the girl never called you is because she's dead, I told him. We don't know that, he said. One of us does, I told him.

Kent told me not to let it get me down. Cases go unresolved like this all the time, he said. He reminded me of the club I once belonged to many years ago when I was living in L.A. There were only two members in the club: myself and the great musician and composer Van Dyke Parks. Both of us had been doing a fairly adult portion of Peruvian marching powder for some time and we both, quite naturally, were rather depressed. The club was called

The Undepressables. Van Dyke and I made a pact that hence forward nothing would ever depress us again. Friends could get sick, go broke, get fired, get divorced, die, kill themselves, kill everybody else, not invite us to their dinner parties—it didn't matter. The club's one rule was that although Van Dyke and I were permitted to depress others, we would not permit anyone or anything to depress us. Finally, we got so undepressed that things started getting depressing so we had to disband the club.

I thought now that I probably hadn't been this depressed since before Van Dyke and I formed The Undepressables. And, of course, I always remembered my father's wise words: "Cheer up, sonny boy. It only gets worse." Yet somehow, the cat, the puppethead, and I still managed to navigate the deep waters of life and the shallow ones, the rough ones and the lonely ones.

It must have been about a year after all this shit had happened that McGovern came into the loft one day with the puppethead squeezed in one large hand and a newspaper clipping in the other. I placed the puppethead back on top of the mantel and then walked over and looked at the clipping McGovern had placed on my desk. It was a small story from the back pages of the *Daily News.* I laughed bitterly when I read it.

The skeletal remains, or skel-ē'-tal remains, as Piers Akerman would say, of an unidentified young woman had been found by workmen in a trunk in the basement of a building at 198 Vandam Street. There was no way to accurately determine who the victim was or how long she'd been there. Well, she's not doing so bad, I thought blackly. The rest of us don't know who we are either, or how long we've been here.

But it was bad enough. Bad enough to haunt your dreams. Bad enough to make you wander aimlessly through the streets of the Village. Bad enough to make you wish you could never want to forget. So I told myself a little story that my old friend, Dr. Jim Bone, had once told me. I told it to myself as if I was telling it to a small child. But really, I suppose, I was only reminding myself that the grief, guilt, and rage would surely destroy me if I didn't let this go.

The story goes like this. There were two monks in the old country who once took vows of chastity and silence. Sometime later, a big flood came to the land and the monks happened upon a weeping woman trapped by the raging river. One monk unhesitatingly picked up the woman and carried her across a narrow footbridge to safety. She said, "Thank you, kind sir," and the monk answered, "God bless you."

Many years passed and the monks were old men and the order relaxed the vows a bit for monks who grew very old. So one day one monk said to the other, "I still remember that day you broke both your vows. You vowed not to speak and not to touch a woman, yet you picked that weeping woman up and carried her across the bridge. I can't believe you carried her across that bridge."

"I can't believe," said the other monk, "that you're still carrying her."

Every time I think of Zarah, I think of this story. Sometimes it works.

ABOUT THE AUTHOR

What can you say about an author like Kinky Friedman? That he's a columnist for *Texas Monthly* magazine? That he's overfucked and overfed and never worked a day in his life? That he's a descendent of Richard, the Ninth Earl of Buttwind? That he divides his time between Martha's Vineyard and the gas chamber? Why do these pretentious bastards always divide their time anyway? There ain't that much time left. One of these nights you might see Jesus doing a dog food commercial. But enough about Jesus. What can you say about an author like Kinky Friedman? He doesn't divide his time. Doesn't live in any city. Doesn't have a wife. Doesn't have two kids named Winston and Kool. Doesn't have a job. Doesn't have a hobby. Doesn't wear underwear. He's an extremely generous Indian giver. He's one of the greatest living writers who ain't dead.

ACKNOWLEDGMENTS

I'd like to thank my editor, Chuck Adams. He's a fine editor, a true author's editor who works in the trenches with writers and manuscripts. He's been with Simon & Schuster for fourteen years, ten of which I've had the privilege of working with him. Without a talented, loyal, experienced, dedicated editor like Chuck, no publishing house can hope to grow or be great. Because that's where it all really starts, an editor finding a manuscript he believes in, shaping it, developing it, and guiding it through the often torturous publishing process.

Over the years Chuck has edited scores of notable authors including Joseph Heller, Mary Higgins Clark, Joe McGinniss, Sandra Brown, Barbara Delinsky, Susan Cheever, and James Lee Burke to name only a few.

Last December, in a supposed "corporate downsizing" move, the powers that be, perhaps in some distant boardroom, let Chuck Adams go, along with his gifted assistant Cheryl Weinstein. Many authors, editors, and agents seemed shocked and angry at this sudden turn of events, but it's really not all that surprising. Corporate thinkers rarely have a notion of who made them what they are or how they got there in the first place. Geniuses like these put Mozart in the gutter, Van Gogh in the cornfield, and Rosa Parks in the back of the bus. Down through history they've turned their backs on everybody from Peter Rabbit to Jesus Christ. Why should anyone be surprised that they fired one of their very best?

Thank you, Chuck. I'm a better writer because of you.